G000113175

ramus [rey-muhs]

noun. Botany, Zoology, Anatomy.
a branch, as of a tree, plant, vein, bone, etc.

1

This is a work of fiction. Names, characters, businesses, places, events, locales, and incidents are either the products of the author's imagination or used in a fictitious manner. Any resemblance to actual persons, living or dead, or actual events is purely coincidental.

2019 First Edition

For Tilly,
you are the gift that keeps on giving and the girl that keeps me living.

Prologue
Tuesday, 7 September 1982. 6:15PM.

The tall man cried as he hugged the limp body. Soundlessly and almost tearlessly he showed his despair. Crying for the child and for himself. The small, beautiful and now lifeless creature hung heavy in his arms. A little girl of only ten years old, she had been no threat. He knew what he had done, and he knew what was going to happen. There was no covering this up. There was nowhere to escape to before they came for him. Her friends had seen his face, seen where he lived and seen what he had done. No, this was not something he could run away from today. He lay her body on the ground and sat down next to her head. Stroking her hair, the tall man looked past the trees, and waited.

Chapter 1
Monday, 20 May 2019, midday

The rain was absolutely torrential, reducing visibility to mere metres. Even with the wipers on full speed, the windscreen barely allowed sight of the road ahead for more than a fraction of a second. Why is it, Jim thought angrily, that car manufacturers see fit to include the latest technology into a car dashboard, which no-one ever uses, yet can't get a bloody windscreen wiper to actually do its job?

Jim began to regret his decision to take this route, an A road in the depths of Somerset. He could have used the motorway and at least been able to stop at the services for a coffee, hoping the rain was short-lived. This particular road, like most country roads in Britain, was full of potholes, mismatched tarmac, and was too narrow for more than one vehicle most of the time. It was also not subject to restricted low speeds—another problem with Britain's Victorian-era hangover.

This latter problem raised its head whilst Jim fiddled with the wiper speed. A Ford Focus, with its headlights on full beam, came gliding round the bend a hundred metres ahead. Jim swore loudly as he squinted. The irritatingly bright headlights caused him to lift his foot from the accelerator. The driver of the Ford seemed far less bothered about the current conditions and continued at a speed more suited to a dry summer's day. Jim's heart pounded involuntarily as he feared the worst, gripped the steering wheel and, pointlessly, breathed in to make himself smaller.

A deafening crack filled the car. The noise was the Ford, clipping Jim's wing mirror and sending it shooting into an overgrown hedge. Jim's ears rang and he could almost hear his own blood pumping. Unharmed but furious, Jim slipped into a tirade of abuse as he realised the Focus was actually a police car, yet clearly had no intention of stopping. Dealing with the damage to Jim's car was obviously far too mundane a task for the Formula 1 Flying Squad.

"Fuck's sake. What the fuck was that? Pricks!" Jim shouted, at no one who could hear, before pulling over to the left and turning off the engine. He gazed through the window at a blur of raindrops, not able to see that his wing mirror was now just a metallic stump. He flicked on the hazard lights and sat upright, head back, eyes closed. This was not how today was supposed to go.

When Jim woke up that morning, in his small Portishead flat, everything was dark and quiet. He was supposed to go to work, but had already texted in as sick, having no desire to go to an office populated by people he had grown to hate. The world, in fact, was populated by people he had grown to hate, but at least 99% of them did not have cause to speak to him—unlike the morons in his drab corporate shoebox. Jim worked as an IT administrator, which everyone knew just meant he turned computers off before turning them back on again. Anything more severe than that and he needed to get a budget code from another office via people he had never seen in person. He hated the job, hated the people, and pretty much hated himself. This was his eighth sick day this year. It was May. Not even half the year gone and Jim was setting himself up for an HR meeting about his 'welfare' and 'wellness', which really meant 'disciplinary'.

As Jim sat in the uncomfortable seat of his ageing Seat Ibiza, he pulled his bottom lip between his teeth. He considered the benefits of staying in this sedentary cocoon until the rain stopped and he could be bothered to move again. This idea was made less attractive by another speeding vehicle flashing past at an uncomfortably close distance. Another Battenberg-coloured police car. Jim hoped the bastards crashed, and then chastised himself for thinking it. He was supposed to have a new mantra of positive words and thoughts. 'Bastards' was not one of those.

Jim's original plan—after texting his supervisor an unnecessarily detailed description of fake bowel problems —was to go to the gym. Or, rather, go to the sauna at the gym and sit there until he got too hot; then have his obligatory morning coffee in the gym member's bar. There was no point in exerting himself with the exercise machines in case some steroid-pumped teenager tried to sell him yoga classes. Potentially, he could have a heart attack, or worse, get bored.

Cranking the key and flicking off his hazards, Jim proceeded along the same route. He no longer intended to head to his original destination. Motivation evaporated along with the rain, and he decided that the gym was no longer where he wanted to be. There were bound to be too many people there. There always were.

Within seconds of pulling away, Jim saw what was undoubtedly a very deep puddle around 100 feet away. A massive pothole filled by the unceasing rain. Sensible actions were quickly dismissed, and he carried on through it, not caring how much water got splashed under his unloved auto. Unbeknownst to Jim, who was far from a car connoisseur, the countryside's muddy water made its way forcefully into the cylinders, essentially flooding the engine. The car carried on for a few more metres before the engine cut out entirely. Running on inertia, Jim pulled the car over to the side of the road again, before letting loose a few more juicy expletives.

"Oh, brilliant. Absolutely fucking beautiful. Well done. Well fucking done. Driving along on moving wheels is clearly in the too-hard-to-do box today."

Jim turned the key to start the engine and was met with the sounds of a car in denial.

The more he cranked the key, the more stubborn the car sounded, and after a few tries he gave up. Picking up his phone from the front passenger seat, Jim unlocked the screen. No signal. The phone landed back on the seat with a dull thud and Jim rolled his eyes.

"For fuck's sake." He said, for it was his new favourite phrase.

Chapter 2

Claire sent another text to Jim. According to WhatsApp, he was online 30 minutes ago and had not yet read her messages. Not a big deal, but she was now in the supermarket queue with the shopping for tonight's dinner and she wanted to know if he was ok with cottage pie. He will bloody well have to be ok with it now, she thought to herself, slightly annoyed but not really sure why. She knew he was at work and could not spend all day looking at his phone. He was usually on it a lot, though. She often looked at WhatsApp just to see when he was last online. He seemed to be rarely offline.

Claire paid for the groceries and put them in her reusable 'green' bag. Bugger paying for a plastic bag when it would only end up in the kitchen drawer with all the others. While juggling the bag and her purse, Claire reached into her back pocket for the car keys. She watched the checkout girl scan the items of the next customer and wondered whether the young *'retail asset executive'* really was as unhappy as she looked. The girl was only about 17, with her whole life ahead of her—full of options and potential—no doubt to be wasted away like most of Weston-super-Mare's young generation. A cycle of young pregnancy, marriage, divorce, marriage again, maybe another pregnancy; followed by an unsatisfying job, welfare assistance, complaining about welfare assistance, drinking, debt and passing the cycle on to her offspring. Evolution in action.

Claire smiled at her cynical thoughts. For all she knew the girl could be saving money before going to university and studying medicine. She could end up winning the Nobel prize for cancer research in twenty years. Or not.

Realising that her keys were now free from the debris of her too-tight pockets, Claire wandered out past the trolleys and into the car park. There were a lot of empty spaces near the entrance and she wondered why she'd chosen to park so far away. Especially with this torrential rain.

One bag in hand and handbag on head, Claire jogged at a pace barely faster than walking and was pretty much saturated by the time she slumped into her driver's seat. She slipped the grocery bag into the passenger side footwell, the handbag onto the passenger seat and slipped her key into the ignition. The inside of the windows was already starting to steam up, so she set the wipers running and flicked the heater on to full blast, hoping to clear the condensation.

"I'd rather be at work." She said to herself, thinking of the comfy office chair where she designed the artwork for children's books. Her office, unlike Jim's, was bright, open and contained only two people. Claire and her colleague worked on state-of-the-art Apple Mac computers, took long lunch breaks and gossiped incessantly. It was a wonder they managed to meet their deadlines. Although today was a weekday, Claire always seemed to accumulate days off and was being forced to take them before she accrued too many and had to forfeit them. As the glass began to clear, Claire reversed her little red Ford Ka out of the parking space and headed home, to the flat she shared with her sister. She would much rather move in with Jim, but he was adamant that they needed space before getting into the serious business of living together. He was far too interested in playing his Xbox to be tied down in a serious lifestyle. At least, that's what Claire assumed. The truth was that Jim would be happy for her to move in with him, but he knew that this would soon lead to moving somewhere bigger and he simply enjoyed the peace and quiet of his own private world.

Arriving home less than half an hour later, Claire dropped her keys on the kitchen worktop and set to putting the food in the fridge. She would take it with her when she went to visit Jim later—as she did most nights— and toyed with the idea of pre-cooking everything so she could spend more time on the sofa with him. She checked WhatsApp again, slightly dismayed to have not yet received a response. She was surprised that Jim's 'last online' time had not changed and wondered what he was doing. She knew that he hated his job and spent more time procrastinating on his phone than doing anything remotely productive. She opened up 'find my friends' to check his location. Slightly stalkerish, she thought to herself, but it was just a bit odd that he hadn't replied, or at least read her messages. The app loaded up, showing her location correctly at home and showing Jim's as on the A369. A frown creased the skin above Claire's nose and her heart picked up pace. Her first though was to call him, but she thought that might alert him to her secret stalker tactics.

Instead, she flicked out a new text message, reading,

'everything ok? You're not usually too busy to tell me what food you want! ;) too late now. I'm making us cottage pie and we can watch American Horror Story later. C u at 7 xxx'.

The A369, she knew, was a road leading out from Portishead, where Jim lived. However, it was not the road he would take to work. In fact, it was in the opposite direction. She wondered, and then immediately dismissed the idea, if he was seeing someone else. Not a chance, she thought, he's far too lazy to go to the effort. That brought a smile to her lips, only briefly, as her self-humour faded into worry. It was just a bit weird, and she hated not knowing why he was supposedly on that road today. She considered the probability that it could be an error on the GPS signal and he was, in fact, in his office. She planned to give him another hour and then she would call him.

Chapter 3

Jim was cold. He was annoyed. He was, more importantly, stuck in a country lane in the pouring rain with no phone signal. What were his options? He could wait until the rain stopped and hope that somehow, magically, the signal returned along with the sun. Not likely. So, that option was not an option and he was just making himself angrier. The only real option was to get out and walk to a place with either signal or a phone. That meant getting very, very wet. He looked in all directions, trying to decide which way would involve the least amount of walking. Not that it really mattered. Approximately five seconds in this rain would drench him through to his core. He slid his phone into the pocket of his soon-to-be soaking wet jeans and held the car keys in his left hand. In a swift motion, not unlike that of a slightly uncoordinated newborn monkey, Jim opened the door and stepped out onto the road. He stood ankle deep in the huge puddle he had forgotten he was trapped in and cursed his stupidity. He skipped up to the tarmac and jogged to a nearby tree, which provided a small modicum of cover.

This area of road was entirely rural. There were lots of bushes, a few trees, and fields in all directions. There was also, to Jim's surprise, a single house that he had not previously been able to see. From his position in the car, and with the overhanging greenery caressing his bonnet, it was fair to say that he had not been able to see much of anything. He looked at the house, although it was slightly unfair to call it such. It looked more like a stately home.

Bright yellow, oddly, and situated about 200 metres up a gravel path between two patchy, green fields of grass.

There were three-foot-high solid rock walls all the way along the road, extending from Jim's rather sad-looking car until they reached a wooden gate, approximately fifty metres away. The gate was panelled, and although he could not see if it was padlocked, he was certainly confident that he could climb over it if necessary. Surely someone was living there, Jim thought. It might even be National Trust; that would be even better as it meant normal people working there with modern technology rather than some crusty old bint who probably sent messages via carrier pigeon.

Soaked to the skin already there was very little point in running, so Jim walked alongside the rock wall until he reached the wooden gate. As suspected, there was a padlock linking it closed to a post, so he used the panels as a makeshift ladder, and clambered over. He landed on the muddy grey gravel with a satisfying crunch and took in his surroundings. The path was straight and long, leading to what was presumably the house's main entrance. The fields on either side were not really fields, but huge expanses of grass, split into sections that would have been beautiful gardens once upon a time. Trees filled the far edges with bushy but fruitless branches. It looked typically old-Britain — a throwback to a time when the UK was important. Nowadays, of course, the UK was just a small island generally disliked by the rest of the world, and those families who once proudly owned houses like these were fast becoming an oddity, rather than a regular feature of the countryside.

The house, or mansion, seemed even bigger now he could see it properly. Its front entrance, albeit a very large, chunky wooden door, was enveloped by an arrowhead shaped arch jutting out in front. On either side of the entrance were an equal number of high, vertical, rectangular windows with lead-lined markings, six in total, reaching the edges of the building. The house looked as though it was two main storeys high, although an arched roof probably contained a set of large attic rooms. There were two chimneys, with smoke pluming from neither. There was also a distinct lack of light or activity apparent from each window. It might be daytime, but the sky was stormy, grey and almost entirely cloud-covered. There were no cars parked in the front driveway area, and—most frustratingly of all—no signs indicating it was part of the National Trust. If the grounds were not so well-maintained it would look abandoned and lifeless.

The gravel path connecting to the open front driveway split into paths snaking around each side of the house. From his distant position, Jim could see that the house went back quite far and there were other smaller buildings, or outhouses, further back to the rear side of the building. These were also unlit and apparently free from activity.

Bowing his head to avoid the rain from getting in his eyes, he stuck both hands deep into his pockets and trudged at a belligerent pace up the gravel path. The crunch of each step hardly audible above the sound of water pelting every surface.

It took about 2 minutes until the rain suddenly stopped tattooing his head. He was stood under the archway, a metre from the door. There was no doorbell. Of course not, he thought, sarcastically. Anything from the twentieth century onwards must be too new for a place like this. A doormat sat on the floor and looked rather out of place, being too small for a door this size and very grubby indeed. There was also an engraved name on an oval plaque: 'Neates House', it read, in a deep cursive font.

A large, black door knocker the size of his head faced him at eye level. He rapped with it twice. No response. He tried again a few more times with a lot more force. Minutes passed with no answer. He stepped back out from under the arch and looked both left and right. Which way now? He decided to walk to the right, along the eastern edge, and made his way round the side of the building, looking in each window as he passed.

Chapter 4

By now, Claire was both worried and angry. One side of her brain decided that Jim was dead in a ditch somewhere and she was panicking about what to do. The other side of her brain—the female, cynical side—decided he was just being a dick and not responding to her. She had now left at least a dozen messages and voicemails, each shorter and sharper than the last. 'Fine', she thought. Be like that. I'm not going to waste my time.

But, she did. She sat down, flicking through the channels on the TV, not paying attention to any of them but grateful to be occupied in some way. The sound of voices from the various programme's presenters, talking about sizzling shallots, parliamentary procedure, or the latest updates from Uzbekhistan only irritated her further. She cared very little for what they had to say. Their inane uttering only got in the way of her thoughts. The ones, of course, that she was not going to waste her time on. She turned off the TV, stood abruptly and picked up her purse. She walked purposefully to her keys, dragged them into her pocket and put her still-damp jacket back on. She looked at her phone again, just to be sure. Its blank screen confirming, almost smugly, that no-one was replying to her today. The hallway echoed after she slammed the door closed and walked out to the parked cars.

'Find my friends' still showed Jim's pulsating blue dot as located halfway along the A369. Maybe there was some team-building exercise going on today, Claire suggested to herself. Some sort of outdoor thing where colleagues formed deep, special, lifelong friendships and workplace trust through moving logs and cones together in a field. Or, maybe he's shagging someone. She set the engine running, flicked the wipers back onto full, and pulled away in the direction of Jim's supposed location.

Jim was indeed still in the vicinity of the A369, although his signal had cut out a few hundred metres before he had eventually been forced to stop. His updated GPS location was slightly inaccurate, as it always seemed to be, but his phone had last registered his 'precise' location only a short way back down the lengthy country road. His car would be easy to spot for anyone who cared to look. They would not, however, find him in it, as he was now at the rear of Neates House still unsuccessfully trying to garner the attention of anyone inside.

There only appeared to be two entrances. One at the front that he had already tried and another smaller door at the rear, which from the window next to it looked to be a very large kitchen. Both doors were locked, and both doors elicited no reaction from anyone who was—or as now seemed likely—not inside. At this point, Jim was thoroughly soaked. His skin felt clammy and water streamed from every piece of saturated clothing. He literally could not get any wetter. He felt as though he could not get any more miserable, either, but knew he had had worse days in the past. He no longer cared about avoiding the rain. He looked out at the grounds from the rear of the property and saw that there was nothing but more fields and trees. Random outhouses and sheds were dotted in the distance, but as far as he could tell they looked unused and empty.

He sat on the edge of a large, empty plant pot and looked down at the phone in his hands. It gave smug confirmation that there was still no signal. He started tapping out a message to his girlfriend, thinking of ways to explain his current predicament, hoping that it would send as soon as some tiny speck of service appeared.

"Can I help you?"

Jim nearly dropped his phone in fright.

"Shit," he said, "you scared me!"

"What are you doing?" A tall man said, who Jim could now see was stood less than a metre behind him. He looked up at the figure and took in the unfriendly features of the scruffy source of the question. The man looked about seventy, although he was probably a lot younger, not blessed with a smooth complexion or youthful glow. He looked a bit like Wurzel Gummidge in Jim's opinion. His eyes were sunken and his eyebrows were like bunches of dark straw. A long, hooked nose completed the facial ensemble, with little tufts of grey hair sticking out of each large nostril. He was wearing an oversized wax jacket, brown corduroy trousers, and plain black Wellington boots.

"Sorry. Just a bit shocked. I didn't see anyone around. I really need to use a phone," Jim replied.

"There's no one in. And if there was, they wouldn't answer the door unless they're expecting someone," Wurzel explained. "I've got a phone, but there's no signal round here."

"I noticed."

"So, you'd better be on your way then."

"My car's broken down," Jim said, trying to elicit some sympathy from the imposing figure standing over him. "I really need to call someone to help. There was nowhere else to go."

"Mm. Well, if you walk a bit along the road you'll eventually get a signal. Only a mile, maybe, and you'll be able to get something."

Jim considered his physical state of saturation and mental state of exhaustion. He looked at the Wurzel, nodded and stood up. Wurzel's face softened a little and he said,

"Look. I'm just over in the shed. You can have a cup of tea if you want. You look freezing."

"Oh, nice one. Yes please, mate. It's Baltic."

Wurzel seemed to grunt quietly and walked away. Jim took this as his signal to follow and shuffled on behind him. They walked into a large shed full of clippers, shears, black bags, lengths of rope, stepladders, coiled wire, hedge trimmers and things Jim did not know the name for.

"I'm the gardener," Wurzel said, as if his surroundings required explanation.

"OK," replied Jim, "Are you cutting the lawns in this weather?"

"No. Waste of time. I'd be creating more mud than anything else. Ground's proper soaked. Sugar?"

"Oh. No thanks. I'm sweet enough," Jim smiled at Wurzel, but the gardener seemed to miss the joke. Tea was poured from a large, clearly old Thermos flask into a plastic cup. It already had milk in, so Jim was glad he hadn't mentioned he preferred it black. Wurzel handed him the cup and began to pour one for himself.

"What's your name?" Asked the gardener.

"Jeff," Jim lied, "You?"

"Gerald."

Gerald put the lid back on the Thermos and sat on a stack of rectangular, garden centre compost bags. He nodded at another stack in offer for Jim to do likewise. Jim sat.

"Cheers," Jim said. "I hadn't really noticed how cold it was until now."

"Not exactly dressed for the weather are you?" Gerald mumbled, more of a statement than a question.

"I was actually driving down to the gym before the car conked out. Rain didn't look so bad when I started."

"Mmm." Gerald replied, looking into his cup, seemingly not a regular social tea drinker.

"Look. It is freezing. But, you won't get any help out here. Best thing for you to do is warm up a bit and just walk until you get someone on your phone."

"Yeah. Will do. Thanks." He suddenly felt incredibly lethargic. The tea was weak and cold, so he only managed to swallow a few mouthfuls out of politeness.

Jim's bones ached, his head felt foggy, and his nose was numb. He wished he was asleep in bed. He wished he had gone to sleep in his car. He began to regret his decision to call in sick this morning. The excursion to medieval England had been a waste of time.

"Right," Gerald groaned as he stood up, "I've got loads more jobs to be getting on with around the estate so

I can't sit around. How about you finish your tea. Have another one if you want. It'll only get poured on the floor. When you're ready just shut the shed door and put the padlock back to hold it shut."

"Alright mate. No worries. Thanks again."

"Waste of bloody time really. You could pull the door off its hinges if you wanted to. I'm surprised we've never had the tools stolen."

Probably because no one ever comes down into the back end of beyond, thought Jim before simply saying, "Yeah. I see what you mean."

Gerald walked out the door without looking back or saying goodbye. He seemed less than concerned with what Jim might do with the tools and more focused on where he was supposed to be. He might be old, but he looked strong and well-built. Probably a perk of the job, thought Jim, plenty of exercise and weight-lifting in a job like this. Bollocks to working outdoors though. Bollocks to work in general, he mused. Jim considered the option of never going back to the job he hated.

Chapter 5

Claire looked at her phone again. It was sat on the passenger seat, sliding around with each stop-start of the car. The screen remained blank; impassive to Claire's concerns and unwilling to ease her frustration with a friendly ping. She drummed the steering wheel with her fingers as she waited at yet another red light. Rain beat her windscreen and made her yearn for a warm blanket. The sound of the wipers desperately flailing at their maximum speed only made their futile efforts even more pathetic. She gripped the gearstick and forced it back into first. *I'm definitely getting an automatic next time,* she thought.

Twisting her wrist, she saw that the time was now two pm. Her thoughts took centre stage. Jim should most definitely be at work, and there are far too many people around for a weekday. She decided that everyone, and everything, was really getting on her nerves today. Clenching her jaw she drove ahead, feeling as though everyone else was driving far too slowly and why were there so many cars today? Probably because it's pouring down, she decided, and no one is stupid enough to walk.

Public transport in the UK, especially 200 miles from London, could never be described as efficient or user-friendly. Buses were infrequent and expensive. Taxis: extortionate. And, the less said about trains the better. In this part of the world, you only got a bus if you really had to. The car was still king. If only the roads were well-maintained and there were some empty parking spaces in *any* location. Claire's mind wandered back to her holiday in

Barcelona last year, and how easy it had been to get around the city. Their underground system seemed miles ahead of anything else she had used. Even Jim seemed to enjoy the travelling around. Usually, getting him to do anything that involved moving his legs was impossible. All he wanted to do was play video games and sleep. In Barcelona, however, he was a different person. He wanted to see everything, and was even enthusiastic about seeing the art and street performers. He seemed to know more about Antoni Gaudi than she expected, although her expectations on that matter were fairly low. He took countless photos of the Casa Batllo, commenting on how difficult it must have been to get the glass and brickwork to curve in such a way.

Thinking about Jim like that made her smile. He was so much more than he let anyone else see. Almost everyone who knew him thought he was grumpy. Funny sometimes, but grumpy nonetheless. He avoided social situations like the plague, and could always be counted on to say, 'maybe' to an invitation then definitely not attend. Some people even thought he was rude because he rarely answered a question with more than two or three words. She knew better, though, and he was actually very thoughtful when you could elicit a response. His responses just tended to be less frequent than other people's.

Another red light appeared in the distance, so Claire slowed down using her gears, hoping that she'd arrive at the lights in time for them to change back to green. No such luck, however, and she was forced to come to a complete standstill again. The lights turned from red to amber—how very considerate—as soon as she'd applied the handbrake. Back into first gear she went. *Definitely an automatic,* she confirmed in her mind. She soon approached a roundabout, which she hated; someone was always in the wrong lane. Making it across without incident, she pressed hard on the accelerator as her car came onto the dual-carriageway. She was halfway along it when her phone made a ping sound. Her heart leapt into her chest and started pounding, although she could not rationally explain why. Checking that the road ahead was still empty, she looked at her phone on the seat next to her and grabbed it. She glanced at the message on the screen:

Your next bill is available to view.
Payment is due on the 1st of the month.
Thank you for being a loyal customer.

"Oh, fuck off."

Chapter 6

Jim looked at his watch, saw that the time was two thirty-three. Taking in a deep breath, he stood up and emptied his tea cup. He leaned against the doorway of the shed, just close enough to see out but far enough in to avoid further soaked feet. He quite liked the emptiness. It was very quiet, aside from the beating of the rain, which he had now compartmentalised in his mind as some sort of soothing white noise. He looked at the trees and wondered if kids had ever climbed them. He knew that he would never have kids of his own. He was far too selfish, broken and lazy for that, although he had not yet told Claire of his feelings about parenthood. He wondered if she felt the same, but knew deep down that she would probably feel her biological clock ticking soon enough. She deserved better than him.

Suddenly, his attention was drawn to a window on the mansion's upper floor. A light was on in the window at the far end. Not a ceiling light, but a candle-lit lamp. As clear as day. He was sure it had not been on earlier, but could not say for certain. He wondered if the gardener had lied to him about nobody being in, or whether he simply had not known. Maybe there was nobody in and he had simply missed the light before. No. He was sure everything had been dark when he had made his initial attempt at grabbing someone's attention. After all, candles were not like electric lights; it had to have been lit fairly recently. Was he going mad?

As if to give him the confirmation he needed, a shadow appeared briefly on the wall by the lamp. Jim could not tell what figure the shadow represented, but it was certainly something tangible that skimmed over the wallpaper. Briefly, he considered running over to the door and banging on it again. Then he remembered Gerald's words: *'Even if they're in, they won't answer the door'*, he remembered the old scarecrow saying. Despondent, Jim sat back down on the sacks of compost, finished his stewed tea, and remembered he had a text message to finish typing. He pulled his phone from his pocket and got back to typing it. He knew Claire would have tried contacting him and he had a lot of explaining to do. This was the longest message he had ever written. It would probably be better as an email, but there was no point in changing now—he was almost done. As he finished, an exclamation mark appeared next to his long and wordy message, with the text *'Cannot send. Try again later'*. He assumed it would get sent as soon as a single bar of signal trickled through his phone's antenna. Hoping that was the case, he slipped the phone into his back pocket. *'Move'*, he ordered his legs, standing up with renewed determination. Time to go. No more procrastinating. Staying in the shed forever was, unfortunately, not an option.

Adding further insult to his already injured mind, he had not accounted for the fact there was a thin wooden shelf directly above his makeshift seat. Upon standing up, the back of his head cracked against the corner of the wood and he immediately bent over in pain. It felt as though his skin had been pinched in a vice. The sharpness of the sensation made him crunch his upper body muscles together all at once and, just for a moment, it looked as though he'd inhaled his own neck. Breathing slowly, he relaxed, and the initial pain subsided into an ache. He touched his thinning crown with his fingers and felt wetness. Given that his hair was already wet, this was no surprise, but this new wetness was sticky. He looked at his fingers and saw bright red blood on both of them. After a few seconds, he felt it trickle behind his right ear and onto the back of his neck. He wiped it away, which only served to make his hand even stickier.

A roll of toilet tissue was on top of a set of shears next to Gerald's Thermos, so he ripped off a hefty portion and held the *welfare bandage* to his wound. Cuts to the scalp, no matter how small, always produced a decent-sized flow of blood. Pressing harder caused another sharp, stabbing pain to envelop his skull. He stood still, closed his eyes, pressed harder and thought about being asleep. Maybe he could sleep standing up whilst in pain and bleeding. Dreams could come true. He removed his hand from the top of his head and peeled the tissue away. Looking at it, he was almost impressed with how red it was. Movie blood is a lot darker than this, he thought, remembering something that was once said about movie blood being made from corn syrup. This was anything but sweet. His fingers smelled of rust and the blood on them was already caked into the creases of his skin. For some reason, he licked the tip of his stained fingers and rubbed them with his thumb. The powdered claret became liquid again and he slowly retracted his thumb, pulling with it a string of red like a bloody spider's web. There was no obvious rubbish bin in the shed, so he left the tissue on the offending shelf in mini protest at its assault against him. He stood in the doorway once more and looked out at his intended route. His destination was clear, and he was ready to brave the storm. He just needed to borrow a few of Gerald's things.

Chapter 7

Claire was nearly at the junction of the A369, so she flicked open her phone's screen and opened the 'find my friends' app again. She left the screen on and put it on her knees so she could glance down at it frequently. As the blue dot representing her own less-than-accurate location settled into place, she carefully pulled across the junction onto the pothole-filled A road.

Just two minutes along the narrow country road, her Ka passed through a narrow section of road on a blind bend. As she pulled out of the curve she saw a huge puddle on her half of the carriageway. She was glad to have been going slowly as, lacking visibility, she would have gone careening through it if she was moving at any sort of speed. She took her foot off the accelerator and rolled over it at a turtle's pace, using the inertia of the vehicle. It was deeper than it looked and her poor little car groaned with the suspension's effort. Once through this *dastardly* trap, Claire looked ahead—as much as the rain allowed—and saw that there was a black vehicle at a standstill not too far in front. She drove up to it and pulled in behind. The number plate confirmed what she almost did not want to find. It was definitely Jim's car, and this was still the last location of his mobile phone. She squinted through the windscreen, and with each passing swipe of her wipers had a split-second of visibility. She used each of these moments to examine the car in front, looking for any telltale sign that Jim was sitting inside. His lights were off, and it seemed that his engine was too. The windows were closed and no one was sitting upright in the seats. Maybe, she wondered, he's sleeping in the back. Maybe he got sick or the car broke down and he decided to have a little power nap? Weird, but possible, and if true she would most certainly give him a piece of her mind about it. Picking her phone back up, she decided to call him and see if he was actually in the car. She brought his contact up on the screen and pressed the green call button. No signal. She felt both relieved and annoyed. Relieved because that answered the question about Jim's lack of contact, but annoyed because she could still not contact him. She had very little choice left but to get out of the car and have a look.

Claire pulled her jacket from the back seat, awkwardly pulling it on whilst wedged between the seat and steering wheel. She zipped it up, checked the road again for any other signs of life, saw there were none and opened the door. She got out fast and slammed the door shut. Gracelessly running the five steps required, she peered into the windows on the driver's side. No one was sleeping in the back seat, and there was no one hiding in the front either. Dismayed, she ran back to her car and got in.

It had only taken about fifteen seconds of exposure to become thoroughly soaked. Her jeans were now a much darker shade of blue, and her jacket—which had been so comfortably dry a moment ago—may as well have come out of a washing machine. She looked along the road for some cover. There was a tree on the other side, which although bare of leaves, was still full of enough branches to give a little respite if she really needed to stand outside. What were her options? Option one: go home. That was pretty appealing right now, despite her growing concern. Option two: look for Jim, despite not having a clue where he might be. Option three: wait, and hope he came back. Option four: drive to a police station and report him missing.

She decided on option three. It required the least effort and was the only one that seemed to make sense. She turned off the engine and tried to settle back into the seat. Her mind was racing with possibilities. Where the bloody hell was he? It's quite literally the arse-end of nowhere. No shops. No houses. No streetlights. No pay phones. No Pub. A nice, warm, old-fashioned pub. That would be wonderful, Claire thought to herself, subconsciously avoiding the reality of the moment.

There were a number of fields that she could see and not much else. Her windscreen now made the outside world look as though it had melted. The rain continued to batter the glass, but had settled itself into a greasy, jelly-like coating through which the world took an unrealistic shine. A car approached, and its headlights refracted through the rain covered glass temporarily blinding her. She heard the splash of muddy water strike her doors as the offending vehicle speeded past. Far too quick for this road, she thought. They could kill someone going into a blind corner at that speed. Claire was a bit of a rule follower.

Since turning the engine off, the car windows had become foggy as well as visually impenetrable. Claire played noughts and crosses against herself, drawing childish lines with her finger on the misted glass. She then started doing her signature with her fingernail until there was no longer enough space. It was starting to get gloomy.

The afternoon sky began to darken, quickly, as it transformed into evening. Claire looked at her watch and saw that she had been sitting there for almost two hours. A grand total of four cars had driven past, all going too fast, but none contained her boyfriend. It seemed to her that, if Jim had been at this location hours ago and not yet returned, it was unlikely that he was about to appear any time soon. With that realisation, she went back to her options list and picked door number four: the police.

Chapter 8

Jim started to panic. A moment earlier there was calmness and serenity in his groggy mind. Now, however, he rapidly felt the pressure in his lungs increasing. Breathing was impossible. The grip around his neck was unbreakable and the lethargy of moments ago was evolving into an adrenaline rush. Darkness receded in slowly from his peripheral vision, and he tried with all his might to break free. His lizard brain took over. Fight or flight. He kicked his leg out at the gardener's stepladder less than a metre away, trying to gain some sort of leverage. The oxygen to his brain was completely cut off now due to the force placed on his carotid artery. Darkness came faster, taking over completely.

Chapter 9

As Claire pulled up to the kerb outside the quaint old police station she could see part way down the alley leading to the police vehicle car park. She caught sight of two PCSOs smoking cigarettes under a plastic shelter. She could not quite explain why, but this image irritated her, as though they were somehow not supposed to smoke or take breaks. She assumed she was just feeling irritable in general now, and everything was starting to annoy her. The rain was incessant and Claire really did not want to get wet again so she looked for a more covered parking spot. The entrance to the police station had steps on one side and a ramp on the other. The side with the ramp was also covered by a sort of makeshift plastic ceiling, presumably because people in wheelchairs were not allowed to get wet.

She tried to put such antagonistic thoughts out of her head as she pulled the car next to a tree. She was now about five steps away from the start of the rain-shielded ramp, which was as close as she could possibly get. Nervous at the prospect of talking to the police, she began rehearsing the conversation in her head. *Who was missing and for how long? Would they think she was being ridiculous? Would they give her a ticket for wasting police time? Is it possible to waste the time of people stood outside under a rain shelter, smoking and laughing with each other?*

That last thought made Claire roll her eyes in exasperation at her own continuing negativity. She opened the door and ran to the slope. A satisfying blip came from the car as she remotely locked the doors.

It smelled damp as she entered the foyer of this undoubtedly old police station. Everything looked dated. There were old posters hanging on the wall encouraging you to either go into rehab or be an informant. A set of wooden benches lined the wall, clearly designed to be as uncomfortable as possible in the hope that people got numb arses and walked away before they got their turn at the front desk. The 'officer' manning this particular front desk was similar in appearance to a Scotch egg: round and orange.

The officer was rotund, to say the least. She was wearing a white shirt, although it was hard to imagine shirts in her size ever being considered suitable for a police officer. She had short, frizzy, orange hair, offset by blue plastic earrings and unflattering, round glasses. Claire had visions of this officer jumping on a hardened criminal, screaming at them to give her the chocolate back. *It was her chocolate, God damn it, and she'd fight anyone for it.* Claire used her inappropriate humour to force a smile onto her face.

"Hello," she said, trying to get the egg's attention.

"Yes, how can I help?" it replied.

"I need to report a missing person," Claire said, and noticed the creature's name badge. It read, 'Police Staff E Johnson'. *E for Egg, maybe*, Claire pondered.

"Let me take some details. What's your name and date of birth?" Asked Johnson.

Strange first question, thought Claire. This isn't about me. Nevertheless, she gave her details, along with her phone number and address when the officer requested them.

"Right. So, who's missing?" Asked the egg, who Claire now realised was not a police officer, finally getting to the important part.

"My boyfriend."

"When did he go missing?"

"Today. A couple of hours ago," Claire said, realising as soon as the words came out of her mouth that she was sounding a bit mad. Police Staff Johnson put down her pen and looked at Claire.

"That's not a long time. Is there anything that makes you think he's gone missing? Where would he normally be at this time?"

"Well, normally, he's at work," Claire replied, realising that this sentence had not helped her cause. "But," she continued, "he hasn't been responding to any calls and I found his car abandoned on the road nowhere near where he works."

"Oh, right," Johnson said, slightly more interested, "I'll need to put a report on, and a police officer will need to speak to you. Bear with me."

The officer walked away from the window and sat at a desk. She picked up a telephone and dialled. A few seconds later, she started talking, using phrases like 'delta', 'misper', 'guardian reference' and 'domestic relationship'. After only a minute of this, she put down the phone and returned to the window where Claire was patiently stood.

Johnson began speaking, "OK my love, this is what needs to happen. They're putting a log on the system and a police officer will come here to take details from you. There's no one in right now, but they've called someone to come to you. Are you ok to wait?"

Claire did not think she had much choice, so nodded in the affirmative, which set the officer off speaking again.

"Just take a seat and someone will come and get you. OK?"

Claire nodded again and walked to the uninviting pew. She sat on the hard wooden surface and instinctively started looking at her phone. No messages. She opened the Facebook app and scrolled through a series of everyone else's fake-happy photos and *inspirational* quotes. Nothing seemed real. No one was really as happy as they looked on social media, and as for those inspirational quotes on a background of trees and sun: nobody talks like that. If any of Claire's friends actually started talking in the way their Facebook and Instagram posts read, she would probably call them a retard. She remembered life before Facebook, Instagram and Twitter and thought that things were better back then. Nobody tried so hard to impress everybody else. The selfies, captions and one-upmanship that was ubiquitous today simply did not exist ten years ago. Claire was sure that trying so hard to look happy actually made people more depressed. She wondered how many family feuds, divorces and legal battles had been caused by the virus of social media.

In spite of these thoughts, Claire was an addict like everyone else. She had two Instagram accounts and a Facebook. One Instagram for her personal life, which was really an edited, filtered, photoshopped version of her life. The other for her artwork, with each post accompanied by about fifty hashtags trying to garner attention. It actually made her feel temporarily happy when she got lots of 'likes' and new followers. It was also a source of disappointment when an illustration she had worked really hard on did not get any comments. For what? Claire thought. I will never meet most of those people and I'm not selling anything. I'm literally wasting my time. Everybody is literally wasting their time tapping a glass screen instead of looking at the people that really matter. How well did she know ninety-nine percent of the people she was 'friends' with on the internet and why did she bother to look at their version of a life they didn't really have? She had read numerous news articles about people driven to suicide because of social media bullying. Jim was obsessed with reading the latest news on Twitter, which was almost always about poverty, violence, corruption and despair. It made him angry, which made her angry, because she wondered why he cared so much. Why care about people ten thousand miles away when you can't do anything about it? In fact, she could not really understand why anyone cared about things we have no influence over. People are strange.

Claire's thoughts were interrupted by the sound of a door opening next to her. She had not even noticed there was a door there. It was a wooden door, the same colour as the wall, also covered in posters. As it opened, she saw a man step half into the foyer and say her name. She stood up in response and shook the man's extended hand.

"My name's DC Jain. Come through," he said, opening the door as wide as it would go. He gestured to a chair behind a desk and asked Claire to take a seat. She sat in the chair; it was one of those old-fashioned, grey, itchy-fabric office chairs. It was also quite scruffy with some of the seat stuffing poking through holes around the side. The desk had also seen better days, with scratches, ink and coffee cup rings all over it. There was a computer on the desk, which was a throwback to the 90s. A big rectangular box, upon which a chunky monitor stood. Claire had a computer like this when she was a teenager, although she now used an unnaturally thin, aluminium Mac that made the officer's computer look positively antique. She could even hear the crunch of a hard drive inside the ageing relic.

When both Claire and DC Jain sat down, she looked across at the officer and was surprised at how young he seemed. She guessed his age at between twenty-five to thirty at most. He was clean-shaven, with smooth cappuccino skin. She guessed he was of Indian descent, but sounded very local. He was not wearing a police uniform. Instead, he was dressed quite smartly in a long-sleeved, checked shirt and dark tie. He had a black notebook in one hand and piece of A4 paper in the other.

He placed both on the desk in front of him. She could see the onset of a five o'clock shadow on his strong jaw and wondered if he was due to finish his shift soon.

"So, from what I've read, your boyfriend went missing today sometime between two and three?" He asked, part question, part statement. He did not look at her as he spoke, but started typing on the computer's keyboard with slow, deliberate, single-finger swipes.

"That's right," Claire replied. She felt suddenly nervous, as though she was being interviewed as a suspect.

"I don't really know what's going on, but he was supposed to be at work. He hasn't answered any calls or messages and his car was abandoned in the middle of nowhere. I can't see any reason for him to stop there."

"OK," DC Jain responded, although he continued to look at the computer. From Claire's position she could see that he was filling in boxes on a computer program that looked like it was designed for Windows 95. He suddenly stopped typing and looked Claire in the eye.

"Let me tell you what's going to happen. First, I need to get as much information as possible from you. Then, I'm going to check around the police stations and hospitals to make sure he hasn't been in an accident or arrested for something. That shouldn't take long. After that, I need to check where he's missing from. Do you live together?"

"No," Claire responded, "He lives in Portishead and I live in Weston. He was supposed to be at work and I was going round to his after."

DC Jain nodded as she spoke, but looked slightly confused. He then turned back to the computer and started asking a series of seemingly irrelevant questions about their relationship, his address, his work, phone numbers, friends, description, if she had a photograph, if he had mental health problems or drug dependency. Claire was surprised at how few questions she could fully answer.

"OK," DC Jain said, again. He liked that word.

"I've put on a report and I'll give you the reference number with my details. For now, I'm going to do some checks and I'll come back to you. Obviously, if you hear from him before I do, then call us on this number and give the call taker the Guardian reference written on there. Go home and see if he turns up at yours. Try not to worry. Most of the time these things are just a case of miscommunication."

Claire was not convinced by DC Jain's obviously recycled speech. She looked at the piece of card he had given her and saw the switchboard phone number, a 'Guardian number' — whatever that was — and DC Jain's details, indicating that his name was actually Sajid Jain, Detective Constable 3119, based at Tyntesfield station.

Claire stood up and Jain opened the door again. He held it open, smiling weakly as she walked through it.

"Thanks," Claire said.

"Let us know if he contacts you," Jain repeated.

Chapter 10

As the door closed shut, Sajid Jain sat down at the desk and looked at the screen. Normally, missing people were not initially investigated by detectives. The leg work was done by regular police constables until such time as it became something more serious. However, Jain had been sent down to the front office by his Inspector, who believed the abandoned car made it something unusual and increased the risk assessment accordingly. Jain agreed that this was rather unusual. Boyfriends went missing all the time—often after an argument or alcohol—but usually turned up the next day. This was strange because of the vehicle. Why would the boyfriend leave it in the middle of nowhere?

Tapping at the keyboard, Jain brought up the details of the car's supposed location and wrote it down in his pocket notebook. He scribbled down the girlfriend's phone number next to it, followed by both of their home addresses. He hated leaving the office if he was honest with himself, and that was part of the reason CID appealed to him. He did not really think such mundane tasks were part of his remit, but he was certainly not going to argue back with an Inspector. Despite Claire's assumptions about his appearance, Jain was actually only at the start of his shift. He still had at least seven more hours to go. The rain was still relentless, which made the prospect of a trip to the countryside especially unappealing. Jain looked out at the flooded gutters and decided an umbrella would not do him much good, so he walked through the front office and out of the exit, jogging swiftly to the unmarked burgundy police vehicle he had managed to borrow for the day.

Traffic was heavy and slow, as expected in the conditions, so it took almost an hour to reach the point of the A369 where the missing man's car was supposed to be. There it was, just as the woman had described. Jain drove slowly, and idled closely up next to it with his windows a few inches from the driver's door. The rain was finally starting to slow down, so he lowered the window and tried the other car's door handle. Locked. As far as the detective could see, there was no one in the vehicle and nothing particularly unusual about its appearance. No suitcases on the back seat, numerous clothes or bottles of alcohol to indicate that someone had been planning to use the vehicle as a retreat from an overbearing partner. Police checks showed the vehicle was insured and registered to the missing man, James Lockedon, and the address matched up. Jain had not really expected to find anything here but it was part of the procedure he had to follow for any missing person's investigation. He pulled his vehicle to the side of the road and started updating his notebook.

As he was writing the time on the page, he looked further past the car opposite him and saw Neates House in the distance. He had visited the estate once before, years ago when he was new to the force. There had been a call from the occupants reporting a burglary, although when he attended and spoke to them they explained that nothing had been stolen. The occupants were an elderly couple, who seemed convinced that someone had been in the home without their consent. When pressed as to why, they explained that things felt different. The old couple were both quite eccentric, so he tried to reassure them that there was nothing he could do without evidence of a crime but that he would check the grounds for them to make sure there were no nasty people about. He and his more senior colleague had then spent an hour walking around the massive area attached to the estate, poking around in outhouses, sheds, and unused stables. As expected, there were no people there. Just grass, trees, and rusty equipment to show that there had once been a lot more to Neates House than just two lonely, old pensioners. There had probably been a large family living there at some point, and a team of staff to take care of them. He relayed his findings back to the old couple, whose names he could no longer remember, and never saw them again. He wondered if they were still alive. Technically, house to house enquiries would be part of the investigation here, and although this was the only house for quite some distance there was a small chance that someone inside had seen James Lockedon today.

Moving his vehicle up to the entrance gate, he saw that there was a padlock in place. Disappointed to be undoubtedly getting wet, he pulled the car as close as possible and got out. The skies had slowed down to a fine drizzle now, rather than the power shower of earlier. A decent soaking was still inevitable; Jain's motivation matched his desire to endure it. He climbed over the rungs of the gate and made his way up the path. By the time he reached the front door, feeling damp and listless, some memories of the old married occupants had returned. He remembered that they were very well dressed in old-fashioned clothes, but had a musty funk about them. The woman had done most of the talking, with the elderly gent just nodding along with her. Maybe they were still here. They would probably not remember him, although if they received as few visitors as he suspected, they might do. He used the heavy knocker to bang the door. Waiting for a response he stepped back to survey the windows for signs of life. No lights on, and no movement as far as he could see from the front of the building. No one suspiciously twitched at the curtains, peeping at his intrusive attendance. He knocked again but, rather than wait any longer for an answer, immediately began to walk up to the east edge of the property. Again, memories came back to him as he rounded the building, bringing back details of his search for the mystery burglars. It felt strange to Jain that, many years apart, he would be doing something almost identical: walking around the grounds looking for someone he did not really expect to find. He saw the same old set of stables, sheds and outhouses in the same locations and the same state of tatty upkeep. He also saw the same absences: an absence of life and an absence of light.

As he came around to the rear and approached the back door, he noticed how suddenly darkness had crept up on him. Dusk was sucking up the natural light, so he pulled out his pocket torch. The small beam shone to the far side of the estate. It was only the evening, and it was spring, but the weather had been grey since morning so it was unsurprisingly bleak now. A few knocks on the door and adjacent windows, more for posterity than in genuine expectation, along with some customary sweeps of the torchlight up and down the brickwork. He looked like a proper detective doing some real detecting, thought Jain, with a wry smirk. Eventually, the detective started looking away from the house itself and towards the other small structures dotted around the rear. Another memory flashed back, but this one was not of Neates House. Instead, a memory of police training school popped up like a projection in his mind. Jain vividly remembered a course on domestic violence and missing persons, whereby the trainer had shown them some photos from a real case.

This case involved a young woman who had reported domestic abuse to the police on numerous occasions but her abuser was never arrested. One day, she was reported missing by her family, so the police went to her home and spoke to the husband. He confirmed that she had gone missing but did not know where she was. Days later, after the case was escalated up the police ranks, her body was found in their shed, almost folded in half, legs sticking up from within a refuse bin. She had been there in that exact position when the officers first went to speak to the husband, but as they had not done any checks on the property her body went undiscovered for almost a week. Days of agony for the family not knowing what had happened. Days of degradation and lost evidence due to body decomposition. And, days of opportunity for the husband to get away. Fortunately, he was arrested and ultimately imprisoned, explaining that he had beaten her in anger until she had stopped moving. He had panicked and hidden her body in the shed. When the police came round he almost confessed to them, but when they left without finding her he gained confidence and thought he had gotten away with it, but did not yet know what to do with the body. It turned out that he had beaten her on many occasions and she had been failed by the authorities—the police—who could have prevented her murder. The memory of that case, and the photos in particular, had always stuck with Jain when most other legal definitions and case law had long since been forgotten. For that reason, he looked at his surroundings now and realised that if he did not look in all of them, then he might be failing someone.

Jain started with the old stables, methodically opening and looking in each. They were all just empty concrete shells. He moved on to the sheds, and found them all empty except one. This shed was most certainly not a lifeless, empty shell. In fact, it looked positively homely. Aside from all the tools and gardening equipment, there were other items that the detective considered odd for that location. There was an oil lamp on a shelf, unlit, but quite new looking—and a massive fire hazard, he thought. There was a thick blanket, folded up and neatly placed atop a stack of sealed compost bags. There was a Thermos flask, with tea still inside, on a different shelf, and a carrier bag with some sandwich wrappers on the floor. The use-by date on the sandwiches indicated they had been purchased at least three days ago. Jain also noticed a red stain on the corner of a shelf near the doorway. Jain used his phone camera, and handy flashlight, to take a photo of the belongings before inspecting the red stain more closely. He had seen enough blood in his time to be fairly sure that was what it was. His gaze drifted vertically down from the shelf and he saw spots of red on the floor beneath it. He took another photo and walked back out of the shed.

The rest of the area was pretty much just grass and trees. Big old trees lined the perimeter, going back as far as the low light allowed him to see. He decided there was nothing more he could do here and it was time to leave. Trees couldn't tell him anything.

Walking back down the gravel path to his car, he saw a man stood next to it, looking in the window. He stepped off the noisy gravel and onto the quiet grass, quickening his pace. Just before reaching the gate he shouted, "What are you doing?"

The man stood bolt upright and swung around. Far on the wrong side of middle-aged, taller than average and wide-eyed, the man opened his mouth as if to respond, but ultimately stayed quiet. His eyes flicked to the left and Jain thought he might start to run away, but instead stood still and silent. Curious, the damp detective climbed the gate, before speaking again.

"Who are you, what are you doing and why are you here?"

"Nothing." Said the man.

"That's not really answering my questions. Let's start again. My name is Detective Constable Sajid Jain. What's your yours?"

"I don't really have to talk to you if I don't want to, do I?"

"Well, that depends," Jain responded. "If I suspect you've done something wrong then you most certainly do have to tell me your name."

"I haven't done anything wrong." The man said, sheepishly.

"But, if I suspect you have, and you don't tell me who you are, then I will have to arrest you. And that means you'll be stuck with me for hours down at the police station, which is pretty miserable for both of us, eh?"

"Have you got any ID?" The man replied, with a confused look on his well-lined face. Jain took out his warrant card and showed it to the man, confirming he was indeed who he said he was.

"I'm Gerald."

"And?"

"And what?"

"And what indeed. And, what are you doing?" Jain was running out of patience with this weird guy.

"I'm the gardener. I wondered whose car this was. Why it was in front of the gate." Gerald explained, at last.

"So, do you know where the owners are? Is anybody home?" Jain asked.

"No. There's no one home. They're on holiday. I just do the gardens for them."

Jain thought back to the elderly couple whom he had met many years ago and was not convinced they were the sort to still go on holidays beyond their front door. He decided that Gerald was too strange for his own good and wanted to know more.

"Do you have a key to the house, Gerald?"

"No. Just the shed. I don't need to go in the house."

"When are they coming back?"

"Um. Not really sure. Maybe a week or two."

"Didn't they tell you when they were coming back?"

"They don't tell me much. I just do the gardens"

"I went into the shed, Gerald. Have you cut yourself recently?"

"Oh, yeah, I'm always cutting myself by accident. All the tools and that," said Gerald and showed his hands, which were indeed scarred around the fingers in various places.

"Recently, I said. Have you cut yourself today? There's blood in the shed."

"Oh, yeah, I scratched my finger"

"On a 6 foot high shelf?"

"What?"

"A shelf. There's blood on a shelf and on the floor."

"Yeah, I banged my head. I'm clumsy like that."

"Can I see?" Asked Jain, beyond frustration with this supposed gardener.

"It's just a little nick on the head." Gerald replied, bowing his head to show a greasy mop of grey and black hair. Jain could not see anything to indicate an injury but was not in the mood to go digging around this man's follicles.

"Alright. Alright. Fair enough. Anyway, I'm here to ask if you've seen someone who's been reported missing.

His name's James. Male, 30 years old, about six foot tall, medium build, short hair. Have you seen anyone like that today?"

"No." Gerald quickly replied.

"Are you sure? Have you seen anyone around here at all?"

Gerald sounded certain. "No."

Jain frowned. "Maybe another worker. A postman. A salesman. Have you seen another human today?"

Gerald looked directly into Jain's eyes and repeated, "No. No one has been here except me for days. There haven't been any postmen and I'm the only one working on this estate. Sorry I can't help."

Jain looked at the tip of his pen, firmly pressed against the paper, poised to imprint wisdom, yet it remained in the same static position on his notebook. The ink was bleeding a large black dot on the page, which was about as useful as this entire conversation. He clicked the pen, flipped the notebook closed and put both in his shirt pocket. He thanked Gerald, trying his best to hide the sarcasm, and opened his car door. As he sat back behind the steering wheel, he watched the old gardener unlock the padlock on the gate. Strange, thought Jain, that he was so careful to keep the padlock on the gate in constant use yet the shed full of tools had been left wide open. 'Strange' was the word of the day for Detective Constable Jain.

Chapter 11

Gerald's heart was pounding so hard it felt as though a heart attack was on the way. What the hell were the police doing here? How had someone reported the man, Jeff, James, whatever his name was, missing already? How did they know he'd been here. What if the detective had arrested him? Searched him? Taken him away? It didn't bear thinking about. That sarcastic Indian copper didn't know anything and had no reason to come back. Jesus, he should have just walked away and left that guy alone.

It's too late now. He had a body to get rid of.

Chapter 12

Claire had called everyone she could think of, but had only succeeded in making things worse. Jim's friends, that she knew of, had not seemed too worried. They told her that he had always been moody and prone to going off by himself. He disappeared early on every night out with them, so his random absences and lack of communication were nothing new. Typical men. His parents, however, were beside themselves with worry and asked more questions than she had. She ended up passing over the details of the police officer from earlier along with the police reference number and they were planning on calling him to offer their help. They were such lovely people, Jim's parents, she felt bad for them. Jim was not the best son. He rarely kept in touch, and usually went round to see them only when Claire suggested it. She did not know why he was so averse to it, but assumed it was just part of his introverted personality. Nevertheless, his parents were always checking up on him, making sure he had enough money, buying things for his flat. He was almost rude in his lack of gratitude. She wished her own parents were as generous as Jim's were to him.

Claire considered posting something on Facebook, but decided better of it. Rather than genuine concern and help, it would probably just be an opportunity for people to say the usual niceties and then gossip instead of being productive. Any opportunity to watch a car crash in progress was a human addiction. People she barely knew would secretly relish the distraction from their own meaningless lives and turn it into a joke when Jim inevitably turned up safe and well.

Sitting at home made Claire feel useless. Jim was obviously somewhere, and she was more than a little angry at him for making her feel this way. He had driven out there for a reason and she needed to know why. Determined to get the answer and feeling aggrieved somehow, anger forced her into action. Before thinking of a real plan, Claire was back in her car and heading to the A369 for the second time that day.

The journey was much quicker this time round. The rain had stopped and the roads were clear of traffic. Claire had no clue what she was really planning to do, but just moving alleviated the anxiety a little. Pulling up behind Jim's car, Claire realised she had really not thought this through. She had no torch, no coat, no map, no phone signal and no clue what she was doing here. Jim's car's doors were all locked and she could see no magical handwritten sign inside telling her where to look next. Two minutes staring into the local, admittedly beautiful, countryside allowed Claire's eyes to adjust to the darkness. There were a lot of trees around here, she realised, as if that was somehow useful. What was useful, to her surprise, was the realisation that trees were not the only large, inanimate objects in the area. There was a house. A massive bloody house! How had she not see it earlier? Torrential rain, causing almost zero visibility, was the answer to that question, but the truth did not diminish her frustration. Claire started walking towards the imposing structure, positive that this was definitely 'a good idea'.

The gate being locked put a slight dent in Claire's positivity, but only for as long as it took her to straddle the barrier and drop to the other side. The crunch of gravel sounded incredibly loud in the dark. The depth of darkness surprised her. It was unusual to have an absolute absence of light pollution. Looking up, she saw countless stars and realised that she had not noticed a sky this clear in years. This was the cost of modern comfort and perpetual visibility.

Unknowingly following in Jain's earlier footsteps, Claire moved onto the grass for a quieter approach. She could not really explain to herself why silence seemed the best choice, but the gravel sounded almost aggressive; truthfully, it was knowing that she had no legitimate reason to be trespassing. Undeterred, she made it to the all-gravel semi-circular driveway framing the front of the massive house. She looked up at the windows trying to detect a hint of light. Nothing obvious. She walked to the far left edge of the lawn and around to the building's western side. More windows wrapped their way around, and all were equally black. Creeping as slowly and quietly as the ground allowed, Claire reached the edge of the nearest window. She peered inside but could see nothing except an empty room; Illuminated in tiny portions by the sliver of moon overhead. It was just about possible to make out the shape of a door frame in the room beyond. There appeared to be nothing else, not even a single piece of furniture. Claire's heart sank. This place looked abandoned.

As if responding to her sudden hopelessness, a sound emanated from somewhere inside. It sounded like the thud of a bag being dropped onto a wooden floor. Then, a quick, rhythmic tapping, as if a tiny tin drummer was beating his drum. Claire's pupils were now so dilated through lack of light that she began to make out more shapes from inside. The door frame was still there, but now she could see past it into an open hallway. The first step of an upward-leading staircase was at its centre, but where it lead was blocked from view by the near room's wall. The tapping sound stopped suddenly, and the only noise that remained was the rustle of branches from nearby trees. The window was locked from the inside and so, presumably, were all the others. Claire saw no reason to break into the house but was overcome with the urge to do *something*.

She walked to the rear of the building and looked around. More dark windows, grass and trees. She looked across the open space, admiring the silhouettes of the farthest trees against the moonlit backdrop. It was so peaceful. Many of those trees had stood their ground longer than most humans on the planet had lived. This excursion had been a total waste of time. She walked along the rear of the building, heading to the east wing. Seeing herself in the darkened reflection of each window, her opaque twin resembled a cat-burglar. It did not take long to reach the opposite edge of the house. Reaching down into the filing cabinets of her brain, looking for an answer to the question, 'what next?', Claire drew a blank.

Chapter 13

As soon as he heard the sound of feet landing on the gravel, Gerald shot to the window and stared. From his vantage point upstairs, in what was once the master bedroom, and in total darkness, he remained motionless. The only detectable movement was the tangible beating of his heart, hammering inside his chest as a result of his fear and confusion. Every step she took raised the feeling of panic in his stomach. His throat was dry and his mind raced.

Gerald felt as though God was still punishing him for earlier misdeeds. Why else would three people come to this house on the same day when, at times, weeks would pass without a single soul invading his carefully crafted privacy. First, the complainer, then, the questioner, and now, the spy. Maybe she was with the police too and the earlier visit had been a red herring. Maybe they really knew what he'd done, but wanted to torture his mind before placing him in chains. Gerald would not give in so easily to their games. He would rather meet his maker, but preferably not the way today's first visitor had done. Gerald wanted to die peacefully, like the old couple who used to live here, sleeping in their beds, accepting that their time was coming to an end.

The Macallisters had been good to him. They knew he was different, but employed him anyway. His horticultural skills were nonexistent at first but, in the years since joining the old couple, he had grown in skill to the point where he really enjoyed being outdoors with the flowers, bushes, fields and trees. Of course, the Macallisters were no longer around to praise him on his work, but he kept going anyway. Pride was a sin, but he felt good about maintaining appearances. The fact that a well maintained set of lawns was enough to keep people from checking on the occupants was a continuing source of surprise to Gerald. Surely, he imagined, people should be wondering where the old folks had gone by now. Yet, every day was exactly the same. No one called in to visit. No family sprang from the woodwork wondering why their inheritance was taking so long to appear. As far as Gerald was concerned, he had inherited the house thanks to his hard work maintaining everything, and for his many hours as a sounding board for the lonely old dear. She loved to talk. Her husband had not been much of a listener, so that task became another of Gerald's jobs.

Eventually, however, Old Lady Macallister talked less. When she did, it was often the same stories, over and over again. The husband could barely hear anything at all, which was probably a blessing in disguise. Gerald did not want their money. He wasn't greedy. He was not even sure they had much left. They rarely went anywhere or bought anything except sparse groceries—another of the jobs Gerald started taking on when he realised that he was now responsible for the running of the house. He just wanted an easy life away from the cruel people of the world. Doing all the little jobs was getting harder, not easier, but at least he had a place to stay where no-one bothered him. His tent was on the grounds to the other side of the northern tree line. He never told the couple he was technically homeless, not wanting anyone's pity. If they knew then they never brought it up. Eventually, when it all got too much, Gerald ensured that the husband and wife never woke up again. They would no longer rely on him. Killing them both was easy, but took its toll on his mind. They slept through the suffocation. Disposing of the bodies was the hard part. He had no way to transport them a long distance, so had to make do with what was in the house.

    The memories flashed through his mind for only as long as it took Claire to reach the main house. He snapped out of his trance before he could relive everything, which was a blessing in disguise. The woman outside was being extremely nosey. She did not knock on the door, though, which was a slight concern. It either meant that she was here to spy on him, or she was blind and could not see where she was going. Probably the former. He watched her from the safety of the dark room as she crept around the front of the house and out of his view. He walked as softly as he could across the hall, past the grand staircase, and into the west facing bedroom. From there, he could see down to the ground below but could no longer fully see the girl. She had pressed herself up against a window on the ground floor directly beneath him. As he watched, patiently and silently, pressing his forehead against the glass to gain any sight of the pest, he heard a thud. It scared the life out of him for a moment, thinking the woman had somehow broken in. Thankfully, it was just the cat, jumping from some makeshift perch in the room next door. He heard its claws rapping on the solid floor as it made its way to him. He fed the cat some scraps a long time ago and it never left. As much as Gerald hated human company, the cat was sometimes nice to have around. Assuming it would one day leave him, he had not bothered to name it. Now, the cat was making too much noise. Just the sound of its steps might be enough to alert an outsider to his presence, and that would not do. The cat must have sensed his mood, as it soon stopped moving and lay still on the floor beside his feet.

Gerald continued to stare at the ground below. A few minutes passed before he saw the spy walking along the rear of the house. He sighed, fed up of this intrusion. He stealthily moved into the adjacent room and resumed his window position. The woman was easier to see now. She was standing still, looking around, probably wondering how to get in. Gerald's brow creased even further in a frown. He did not know what she wanted, but whatever it was, it was not in here. At one point she looked directly up at him causing Gerald to freeze in fear, barely willing to breathe. He knew how black the windows looked from outside, as there was no light in the house tonight, so she could not possibly see him. Nevertheless, his nerves were on edge. Her inquisitive gaze did not last long and her attention moved elsewhere. Gerald stood completely still, furious, for what seemed like hours but was only a few minutes. The woman started walking again, back the way she had come. She walked back down the gravel path and over the gate. Finally, Gerald could relax.

Chapter 14

Detective Constable Jain was nearing the end of his shift. It had been one of his more frustrating days at work. The investigation into the missing person, as simple as it seemed, had hit a brick wall. Hospitals had no record of James Lockedon, nor did the police custody units in his force or adjacent ones. The *misper* did have a criminal record, however, but nothing exciting. There had been a drunken brawl once upon a time, which he was arrested for and ultimately charged with public order. Nothing that helped Jain with his current whereabouts.

He had been recently contacted by James' parents, who were understandably concerned, but could offer no insights into his whereabouts. They explained how it would be out of character for him to disappear and had never done anything like this before. His friends, however, confirmed what Claire had said: he often disappeared on nights out and did not answer calls or text messages. It seemed that no-one really knew James that well. His employer described him as quiet, but sometimes moody and opinionated. He had missed work numerous times, as he had done today, through sickness but they had no idea about his mental state, whereabouts or lifestyle. Other numbers were contacted with equal success: zero-squared. The *misper's* girlfriend had provided the login details for 'find my phone' and it remained as it had all day, or at least its last known position was the same. If the phone had been turned off it could technically be anywhere. Home address checks and house to house enquiries were all negative. There was very little else the police could do at this time. If James Lockeden did not want to be found then he was unlikely to be, unless some new information came to light. The detective logged off his PC and went to the duty inspector's office, knocking firmly on the door.

"Come in."

This tiny office, used daily by at least three different inspectors, definitely had the look of a room that no single-person had responsibility for. The walls were covered from edge to edge in yellowing A4 paper. Each notice was already out of date, relating to procedures and memos from years ago. Officer shift patterns, edited with every available colour of highlighter, adorned the pinboard behind the inspector's desk. The night tour inspector was a woman named Evelyn, or Inspector Thorne to her subordinates. She was tapping away on a keyboard far more proficiently than most police officers did. Jain could see she was updating custody records, which meant writing down reasons for keeping arrested people in custody overnight, although he knew that she could not realistically have visited the cells yet. Usually, it was a generic update aimed only at complying with the law rather than really determining if people needed to be kept in custody. Thorne clicked the mouse and turned to look at the detective.

"What do you need?"

Jain cleared his throat, ready with his prepared speech.

"I've been dealing with a misper all day ma'am. All the standard checks have been done, guardian has been updated, it just needs an inspector's authority to confirm it. Premises checks completed, all negative. Family updated. It was reported by the misper's girlfriend, who seems genuinely concerned, but there appears to be no known history of mental health, drugs or anything to raise the risk assessment further, so it's down as medium."

Inspector Thorne nodded at Jain's recital of a common missing person update. Usually, a misper enquiry started at 'standard risk', not 'medium', but there was no need to change it if work had already been done. Thorne did not really care much about things that were beyond her control. She asked for the reference number and found the record on the computer. She read his update, almost word for word the same as his verbal explanation, input her force ID number and saved the record. As far as she was concerned, a few keystrokes and her job was complete.

"That's all done," Thorne confirmed, "and I'll pass it over to the early tour. There's nothing the night team can do I presume?" This meant that she had no intention of getting anyone else to do any work on it.

"Not really. Bank checks would be next, but we'll need further authority for those and he's not high risk, so that can wait until tomorrow. The parents were incredibly frantic and will probably be in touch with us before we get back in touch with them. The girlfriend as well. They all seemed really worried but couldn't give us anything specific that would bring him up to high risk. No medical issues they're aware of. No history of mental health. He's got money and friends if he wanted to hide away for a few days. Probably turn up by the weekend of his own accord but we need to cover the bases, obviously."

Thorne nodded in agreement, taking Jain's word for everything. She dismissed the officer with a curt thank you before returning to the computer.

Jain could feel something eating away at him. He had not lied to the inspector. He really had done everything that was required of him for a medium-risk missing person. However, the car being abandoned in a rural location struck him as something important. The weirdo, Gerald, had also raised his heckles and created more questions than answers. A blue-collar man with that kind of age and physical appearance, prejudiced as it seemed, usually came back with a record on the Police National Computer. But his name was not on there. He should have asked to see some ID, but Gerald had not been breaking the law so he did not see any need at the time. He also should have taken his address for a voters roll check, but again, it had not been at the forefront of his to-do list. He could do that tomorrow if necessary. These concerns clouded Jain's mind on the journey home, but he still felt confident that the misper would turn up. He was probably having a break for a few days and would come back when he was ready. It was a selfish thing to do, worrying his girlfriend and parents like that, but men were inherently selfish in Jain's experience. In truth, he often thought that all humans were naturally selfish. Very few people he met in this line of work had given the detective any sort of confidence in the human condition.

Chapter 15

Gerald sat with his back to the bedroom wall. The cat rubbed against his leg, more out of hunger than affection. The pressure he had felt in his chest when that nosey bitch was walking around was still there. He knew he could not really live here forever, but he did not want to leave yet. He was sometimes surprised that the water still worked, despite all the red-coloured bills that occasionally dropped through the letterbox. The electricity had been cut off long ago, hence the occasional candles and oil lamps, and the water was always cold as a result. Nevertheless, it was a home. It was quiet. It was better than a tent. It was, until today, safe and protected. Gerald had only one real choice: move on. That choice, though, seemed a tough one to take. The man was gone, the policeman was gone, the girl was gone, and none of them had asked about the Macallisters. The cop had asked about the missing man, but did not really know anything. Maybe no-one would ever come back to bother him again. He knew it was unlikely, but still felt that running away now was a bit premature.

Gerald looked at his fingernails. They were tough, from years of manual labour, cracked and needed to be cut. He pulled a large penknife out from his pocket and started digging the dirt from out beneath them. Then, he used the pull-out, extremely blunt scissors to chop them down to size. The clippings fell to the floor between his knees and the cat bent down to sniff them. It was clearly not hungry enough for that, looked disdainfully at the ageing giant in front, and walked off. Cats were probably the closest animal to humans in terms of pure sass and attitude. They reminded Gerald of women; their disinterest in being near him unless they wanted something felt like a throwback to his youth. He had never been married, never had children, never really had a proper girlfriend—unless you counted the drunken fumbles after teenage cheap-beer sessions before his life had really gone down the drain.

Gerald's grim fingernail clippings were not the only detritus on the floor. The whole house had not been cleaned since he had *inherited* it and it was starting to smell. Dust had formed a thick quilt over most of the hard surfaces and the cat had left its small, brown, packets of disdain in various locations. The bedsheets had gone unwashed and the few utensils in the kitchen that he had ever used were still in the sink, soaking in weeks-old cold water. It was not surprising, really. Gerald had never had to wash anything before. He had never used a washing machine or a vacuum cleaner, not that either of those could be turned on now. When he was young, his mum did everything for him. She was a classic housewife. She did all the chores for the two men in the house. However, he had certainly outstayed his welcome in the parental abode, eventually walking out, never to return, after one too many arguments with his drunken father. After that, he had lived in tents until being incarcerated.

Prison had taught him how to do '*man jobs*' but he had never done laundry or kitchen duty. After being released from prison, he had become quickly homeless, unable to come to terms with the responsibilities of adult life. There were too many rules that seemed so stupid, and how did things suddenly get so expensive? No. A life working under bosses half his age and living in a flat visited by social workers and probation officers was not for Gerald. He had lasted about two weeks outside of prison before he literally disappeared from his old home town. A disappearance that was completely against the rules of his release. It had made him a fugitive. One of the few crimes that you could only commit if you were already a criminal. He even saw his own face on the news once, but the media had long since lost interest in his story. He hoped it would stay that way. If he did not have to interact with people too often, then there would be no problems. It was always their fault, Gerald assured himself.

Chapter 16

Claire was at home again. She could not sleep. Every minute that passed was an opportunity for her brain to create new images to amuse itself. They did not, sadly, amuse Claire. They frightened her, no matter how irrational she told herself she was being. She racked her brain to no effect. Where could Jim be? Her brain was in a state of cognitive dissonance, simultaneously feeling the emotions of *anger*, *confusion*, *worry* and *frustration*.

Picking up the laptop from the table next to her bed, she brought Google Maps up on the smudged screen. Wiping the smudge with her finger only succeeded in making it worse. How was it, she wondered, that there was always a smudge on this screen? It wasn't a touch screen, so what kind of mad, invisible gremlin was going around touching people's laptop screens? More attempts by her brain to distract itself without success.

Her eyes refocused on the webpage as a digital representation of the A369 appeared. It was like a line had been drawn through a green puddle. Aside from the occasional black line and grey-green splat of paint, the area was virtually empty. A quick click changed the view to satellite, and the sterile view of abstract emptiness was transformed into blocks of grass and trees. Prettier, but equally unhelpful. Not knowing what she was actually looking for just frustrated her further. The only place on the map near Jim's car was the house. The dark, abandoned, quiet, stupid bloody mansion. What a waste of time that had been.

Click, pinch and zoom, ad infinitum, but no new ideas emerged. The laptop slipped to the side by her legs as her head fell back onto the pillow. She felt along the duvet for the metallic edge of the computer until her fingers reached the screen. She smudged it again when she closed it shut, gripped it briefly, then shoved it across the bed and onto the floor. It landed with an unsatisfying, soft thud onto the thick rug. Eyes closed, Claire desperately wanted to shut out her own thoughts, yet she was now watching them on the inside of her eyelids. A morbid, private cinema of nightmares. Her emotions continued to conjure dark images. First, coming from the anger part of her brain, she could see Jim laughing, arms wrapped around a woman she did not recognise. Next, to go with her confusion, she imagined Jim in a dark room with no doors or windows. He was laughing at her. Then, from her worried imagination came the most visceral images of all. Jim was bleeding, calling for help, trapped in a ditch next to a field. He had been hit by a car that did not stop and he was slowly bleeding to death, crying in pain and self-pity. Finally, frustration sent her a new nightmare, only this was merely a reflection of the truth: a blank map with a single object, the house. The dark, abandoned, quiet, stupid bloody mansion. Her tears finally came.

Chapter 17

The sun was barely visible, yet Jain was already up.
The grand total of 4 hours sleep barely made him feel
human, but all he wanted was caffeine. As coffee dripped
into the jug, the smell of slightly burnt grounds was
hypnotic. If ever there was a better smell in the world than
fresh coffee grounds, he had never happened upon it.
Insomnia had become an increasingly big problem of late.
Shift work had that effect on most people eventually,
causing lost sleep, irritability and reduced concentration.
All of these were making work increasingly difficult,
although he still enjoyed the job. There was no way he
could survive the rest of the day on coffee alone. His shift
was not due to start until three pm. Full cup in hand, the
sofa called. Napping on the sofa was sometimes easier
than sleeping in the bed. Not ideal, but it was the only way
to boost a worsening ability to concentrate, even if it did
cause perennial back pain.

Slumped on the sofa, Jain placed his empty cup on
the coffee table and picked up his Kindle. Reading usually
helped him sleep. Not that it was boring, but there was
something about the screen that was easy on the eye. The
alternative was the phone or the TV, both of which had the
opposite effect: keeping his eyes open. A few pages in and
his eyes felt heavy. Mission accomplished.

Mornings at home usually consisted of intermittent
naps, punctuated by cups of increasingly bitter coffee.
Eventually, work beckoned, and he began his journey. It
was at this time, on his journey, that he regretted having

such an uneventful existence. Every day was almost entirely the same. Wake up, drink coffee, spend time on the sofa, go to work, come home, repeat. The only thing that changed was the time of each activity. Work was the only place, at least recently, that held any meaning. Everything else in life seemed virtually pointless. Why make friends when you could never commit to a consistent social life? Why have children if you could never be there to play with them? If he was honest with himself, he should probably just buy a camp bed and set it up in the station. It would save on rent. Earning money that he would never spend on anything meaningful. He could save up for early retirement and then repeat his pre-work ritual on a constant cycle, completely eliminating the one thing that gave him any satisfaction.

Finally, he arrived at the station, his church. Hopefully, today would be more satisfying than yesterday. He sat in his car for a moment, eyeing the reddish bricks around the building. Another twenty years of this with nothing else to enjoy about life might prove difficult. A person only had so much energy to give to one pursuit. Things had pretty much gone to plan so far. University, join the police, get experience, get into CID. The next steps were going to be tricky. Getting promoted was not a given anymore. Budget cuts and politics were playing a bigger part in policing than a few years back. There was no room for mistakes, especially if you were not yet part of the 'clique'. Those people were the worst, in Jain's opinion. Sycophantic, arrogant, superficial officers with an eye on shiny shoulders rather than real police work. Of course, getting promoted was something to aim for. The extra power to make decisions and the influence over what work got done, as well as the pay and pension. But, and he was confident about this, the bootlickers would not get any support from their colleagues if the shit really hit the fan. No matter how many friends you make in high places, they will drop you and disavow any interaction you ever had. Police officers were no different to any other profession. Those in charge, and those with aspirations of power, were just as concerned with self-preservation as a corporate banker or politician. Public service was very far from the minds of the most senior officers. Jain was not sure he ever wanted to reach the Ivory Tower of senior leadership. Inspector level was fine for him; still able to get involved in real day-to-day investigations but have some influence over the whole team. He had to make it to sergeant first and had already failed the exam once. He could not seem to remember definitions, especially when it came to traffic law. He also had no intention whatsoever of ever working in a traffic department, which just made it worse when the exam result came through and he knew those were the areas failing him. Who gives a toss about 'use, cause and permit'? You could cause someone to drive a car with bald tires, or permit them to do it. He frankly cared little for the difference. It was the same scene of carnage when the inevitable car accident occurred. Let the courts worry about semantics.

Sighing at the thought of traffic legislation, the weary detective exited his trusty old hatchback. They clicked and creaked in unison with the effort of his body getting out. He took the steps up to the second floor two-at-a-time and counted that exertion as today's only bit of exercise. Exercise was fine, if it was competitive, but sweaty shirts were definitely not. PCs got issued with their own uniform to get sweaty in, yet detectives had to buy smart clothes for work. It seemed unfair. Shirts and trousers were expensive, and so was dry cleaning, yet he still ended up meeting the same blood-covered drug addicts and grubby witnesses as every other department. Living alone on a £35,000 salary was doable, but he really wanted to save money and not have to check his balance at the end of each month to make sure his bills were covered. After tax, massive pension contributions and professional subs, there was little left when bills were factored in. He wondered how people survived on lower salaries. Most of the people he met through his work were on the lower end of society's scale. The middle-classes seemed to rarely call the police about their neighbour's violent outbursts or to report they had been stabbed by a prostitute—although he was sure they had their secrets.

The computer's hard drive crunched as it loaded up the desktop. All the computers in use around the office were making unhealthy crunching noises. Computers were in use pretty much non-stop in a police station. Years of use by multiple techno-dullards twenty-four hours a day. No wonder they were so slow. The force could barely afford to keep the cars running so it was unlikely that new high-spec machines were about to arrive. Finally, the applications opened and he could log into his email. One by one, they flooded his inbox. Interesting headings like 'prison escapee', 'changes to knife legislation' and 'dirty fridge' populated the screen. He bulk deleted anything that was not personally addressed to him and found that only two remained.

The first was about a piece of evidence he had seized at a crime scene. The court case had concluded and nobody was claiming it. The item was a blood-stained sweater, handed over by a robbery victim when they reported being mugged in the street. He remembered it well. A young, drunk, attractive female had been walking home after a few drinks in a local pub when someone threatened her with a knife. The 'robber'—a funny word, he thought—had simply pointed it at her and asked for money. She opened her purse to show him that it was empty of anything but coins, and received a punch in the face for her troubles. The thief still took the purse. It was not the most serious crime that had occurred that week, but it was still a robbery and therefore got a lot of attention from the bosses. As a result, he had done everything by the book: statements taken, CCTV from the street was seized, area searched, house to house conducted, offender description circulated by email and, of course, her bloodied sweater was taken into evidence in case the smackhead had touched it. She handed it over willingly, wanting to help catch the bastard, but was left in a thin, scrappy vest that allowed her ample cleavage to meet Jain's eye. He tried not to stare, but soon realised he was just as much of a creep as his other male colleagues when his gaze kept returning to her chest. He almost considered keeping her phone number for a future date opportunity and then remembered he could actually lose his job for such an unprofessional act.

Coming back to reality, he looked at the second email. This one was about yesterday's missing person, James Lockedon. It was from the communications department, informing him that the misper's parents had been in touch asking if they could have an update. He sighed, as there was no update to give. Hopefully, the bloke would turn up today and save everyone the grief. With that in mind, the next application up on the computer was Guardian. The trusty domain of all things police. Everything was logged on this system: crime reports, missing persons, evidence location, intelligence checks and addresses of anyone reporting almost any type of incident. It was both the most useful tool he used and the most frustrating. It had the potential to make policing easier by putting all the information in the same place, but for some reason had been designed to be the most clunky, unintuitive, slow piece of software he had ever used. It looked like it had been created in the 90s but was, in fact, quite new. An IT contractor had probably charged a fortune to create it, and continued to charge a fortune to fix it.

James Lockedon's details popped into view, and it was clear that nothing had been added since the Inspector signed it off yesterday. Refreshing his memory, he read through it again to see if anything came to mind to help him find the man. He was again struck by the lack of criminal record attributed to the haggard gardener, Gerald. He just looked so dodgy, and acted so shifty, that surely he was known to the police. Time to start digging further.

He put Gerald's details into the system and tried to link it to any piece of information: a traffic ticket, a named witness, an old address or a stop-and-search form. Nothing came up. He decided to go back and speak to him or the house occupants again. Even if he did not know where Mr Lockedon was, he had to be dodgy in some way, and he did not believe that the old couple were on holiday. Maybe they just said that to Gerald to stop him bothering them. He also wanted to make sure Mr Lockedon's car was in a safe spot, considering that it might be there a while. If someone ended up crashing into it, Jain would undoubtedly be the one blamed for not getting it moved.

He walked across to the duty inspector's office, wondering who was in the throne today. Knocking on the door, a gruff man's voice responded.

"Yep. Come in."

"Hello sir, I need a form signed for a misper investigation."

"Alright Saj, no problem, what's the deal?" Asked the inspector.

Saj, short for Sajid of course, and pronounced like Sarge, always gave his colleagues ammunition for a joke. He was a Constable, albeit a DC, and not a sergeant. However, every day, everyone who knew him called him Saj (emphasising it as Sarge) and it had become common for those a bit cheekier to just call him 'boss' or 'guv'. On the streets, it caused a little confusion as the public heard him called Sarge and, with no markings on his clothes to suggest otherwise, assumed he was a more senior officer, therefore bombarding him with their questions. His colleagues did it on purpose to avoid being questioned themselves. "Ask sarge," they would say. Being a bit of a jobsworth also added to the nickname's potency.

"A misper from yesterday," Saj began, "should have been at work, but had called in sick. His girlfriend tracked him on her smartphone app and saw his car was not where it should be. He was also not answering any calls or messages. She drove to the supposed location of his phone and found his car, locked, but no-one inside. He hasn't been heard from since and his phone is either turned off or out of signal. Custodies, hospitals, friends and family checked, but negative on the responses. No houses nearby, except one, which is currently unoccupied. I want to do a financial check to see if he has withdrawn any cash or used his debit cards."

"Sounds a bit strange." the inspector said as he looked at the authorisation form. He signed with a scrawl and handed it back.

"It is a bit strange. I met one old guy, the gardener, apparently, of a huge house nearby. It's the only house for miles. He claimed not to have seen the misper, and claims the house's occupants are on holiday. The only thing was, and it's not based on anything, but he just seemed dodgy. He was a bit shifty. Didn't want to answer questions. But, he doesn't have any PNC record and wasn't committing a crime, so couldn't really push him on anything."

"It is terribly annoying when people don't have a criminal record." The inspector said, without a hint of humour. "Oh well, let me know what happens with the bank checks. We'll have to do media if he doesn't turn up today. Not much else you can do. He's probably cleaned his accounts out and buggered off to Spain."

Jain smiled. He liked this inspector. His name was Inspector Ian Banks, but was happy to do away with the formalities and was known—when inside the station—as Banksy. On the streets, it was strictly 'Inspector Banks' or 'sir', but in the confines of the cop's closed world, he was Banksy. Not only was his name 'Banks', but the famous street artist whose name he shared was also known to come from the local area—the police knew the graffiti artist's actual name, which was not anything like 'Banksy'—so the monicker stuck with the inspector, and he was often seen sticking inappropriate post-it notes on the station walls in solidarity with his subversive, artistic namesake.

Now that the form was signed, Jain faxed it directly to the HSBC processing centre, picked up a set of CID car keys and walked back down the stairs to the car park. Getting into the car, it was clear that the previous occupant was a smoker. Police cars were, technically, a place of work so despite being unprofessional, it was also illegal for an on-duty officer to smoke inside one. That did not stop some people though, especially plain clothed detectives who could drive around without being noticed, happily puffing away. The smell of stale tobacco was sickly, so down came all the windows. He pulled away from the rear of the station and headed, once again, to Neates House.

Chapter 18

Gerald had not slept well. The cat would not stop purring around him and the worry of the day before had not gone away. That stupid man's body was heavy. Not getting any younger, it had been incredibly hard work to dig a big enough hole and bury it. It was not as deep as he would have liked, although the rain had thankfully made the ground easier to dig. He also made sure to throw the bloke's keys and pocket debris back in with him. He was almost caught with them in his possession by PC Plod yesterday. His body ached from the exertion. Muscles he had not used for ages cried at him to remember they were no longer supple and well-maintained.

His lower back pain was bad today. It had started in prison, following an injury, and become increasingly problematic over the past few months, not that he really did much in the way of gardening anymore. That job, now unpaid, had fallen by the wayside. He just liked being outdoors in the fresh air, especially now the house was getting less fresh by the day. Sitting in the shed, he looked at the blood-stained shelf. The policeman had told him about that, but cleaning blood from old wood was an impossible task. He pulled a crowbar from the bag on the floor and wedged it between the shelf and the wall. A few firm cranks and the shelf was free. It landed on the compost bags and slid onto the floor. At that moment, he noticed the blood on the ground, too. Circular drops of red, making an abstract smiley face, mocking him from below. Using the end of the crowbar, he scraped away at them, roughing up the soft wooden boards in the process. He took the shelf out to a large, metal bin and threw it inside. It would need to be burned.

Back inside the house, he started opening and closing kitchen drawers, looking for some matches and lighter fluid. He had definitely seen both in the house before. Typical, that now he needed them, he could not remember where they were. Anger flashed through him and he slammed the drawers shut. He needed to keep a lid on his anger. It was his constant downfall. The bang alerted the cat, whose presence had gone unnoticed until now. It flew out of the kitchen, into the hallway, and ran upstairs, probably worried that it might be the next target. Cupboards and drawers continued to bang, but no lighter fluid magically appeared. An old book of matches was sat next to some tea bags, which was a relief. He took the matches out to the shed with some paper. He poured oil from the lamp onto the paper, turning it into a semi-transparent sheet of grease. Dropping more paper into the bottom of the metal bin, followed by the oil-soaked sheet, Gerald watched the flame spark to life as he slid three of them together across the coarse striking surface.

As they fell into the bin, igniting the oil and spreading a flame across the paper, he was reminded of his childhood. In those days, before health and safety laws, he had enjoyed playing with friends in the woods near his home in Birmingham. Together, they would build makeshift sheds and tree houses, none of which lasted long when the rain or wind came and turned them back into useless, individual pieces of timber. Nevertheless, it was a time in his life that was not all negative. The outdoors, he knew, was the only place he wanted to be. Home, school, and later, work, were all too restrictive and full of arbitrary rules. In the woods, he could be himself, almost.

Even as a child, Gerald was not 'normal'. He did not really have the same emotional reactions as the other children. He never owned a pet, and never understood why the children cried when Robby the rabbit or Tiddles the cat died. He saw the animals in the same way he saw toys: to be played with until they got broken. Granted, the cat currently setting up home in Neates House was a bit different, as it was currently his only source of companionship. And, as a companion, it was perfect. It never talked, rarely made a fuss and certainly never told him what to do. He was happy to sustain it until it decided to leave of its own volition. When it did, he would not be sad. His friends, as children, were far too emotional. They always cried. They cried when their parents shouted at them. They cried when they hurt themselves. They cried when they argued.

Gerald did not understand it. He felt pain and anger when he fell over or got into fights, of course. But, when the blood inevitably came—from a cut knee or bashed nose—he enjoyed it. It smelled like rust and was sticky. He actively encouraged more by picking scabs before they were ready, watching the dark, viscous liquid form lines down his leg. He tasted it. Never did any injury pass him by without tasting the blood that flowed. Other kinds of pain were less enjoyable. Burns, for example, were not fun. He had been burned by his mother's iron when he was small, although he could not remember much about the incident. He was not even sure if she had burned him on purpose. He did not really care if she did. She was probably dead now. What he did care about were the blisters. The memory of those white mounds on his skin, full of pus, with a heat that never seemed to end. He could not help himself, though. Just like the scabs, he would pick at them until they popped, flattened, and the pus leaked out. Quickly, he learned that this was a very different sensation. First, the pus tasted awful, and picking the blisters did not ache like a scab. These hurt like a razor. The pain lasted too long, going on for days before he could use his hands properly again. No, no, no. Blisters were bad, and were not to be encouraged. He had what doctors called 'a phobia' of burning himself. Not of fire, per se, but the idea that he could get burned was a trigger for a severe over-reaction.

As if prompted by his memories of burning, the heat from the metal bin warmed his face. His heart beat faster, knowing he was in control of this dangerous element. He looked down, directly from above, and watched the paper curl into black, charred flakes. The shelf eventually started to take the flame and it slowly turned black from the bottom corner. The fire seemed fragile, as if it might go out at any moment, so Gerald stood watching it with silent encouragement.

As much as he hated the feeling of being burned, he loved the sight of a flame. His brain changed channels again, and he remembered his childhood friends propping abandoned wood and tarpaulin into a shape supposedly resembling a 'den'. They sat under the tarpaulin, laughing and joking and picking their noses. He cannot remember laughing much, but he had on that day. Something about stealing sweets from the local shop and how excited they all were. He could not remember their names anymore, but some of their faces were clear. That evening, as it got dark, the small group thinned out until only two remained. Gerald and one other boy. He seemed to be confident that he could go home whenever he wanted, and his parents would not chastise him. Gerald claimed the same, even though it was not true, but he cared very little about what his parents did as punishment. So, together, they sat under the tarpaulin talking about stealing more sweets and other childish endeavours until darkness took over the den. They could see each other, but only barely, and mostly as moonlit avatars of themselves. The other boy had produced a box of 'Swan' from his pocket. Swan matches, the long kind, which he had stolen alongside his rhubarb and custard sweets. They took it in turns to light one, holding it as long as they could, dropping the embers when fire reached their fingers.

Gerald had not liked this game. It was painful, and reminded him of blisters. But, the other boy, the nameless, unloved rule-breaker, seemed unfazed by the brief burns. Frustrated, Gerald told him that he did not want to play anymore, and was going home. Predictably, as children do, especially boys, he was mocked for being a 'baby' and a 'scaredy cat'. These words were like catnip to little boys, pushing Gerald to feel juvenile anger. He felt like he wanted to cry. He often felt angry, but rarely hate. At that moment, he hated the other boy. Hated him so much that he wanted to hurt him. Instead, he just looked at him, scowling, thinking of something to say that would make the other boy feel just as bad as he did. He could not think of anything, so he pushed him. Shocked, the other boy fell onto his backside. He looked at Gerald with his mouth wide open, and was about to say something else. He never did though, as Gerald kicked him. His fast-rising anger had risen. The end of his toe, encased in a heavy school shoe, struck the boy's open jaw cracking it shut and smashing some teeth in the process. The boy grabbed his face and made animal noises unlike any Gerald had ever heard before. He was so loud. Nasal screams, muffled by a blood-filled mouth, seemed to go on forever.

In panic, Gerald pulled a piece of wood from their den, causing the tarpaulin to drop over the boy, and hit the moving shape beneath. Soon, the boy's head came free: a dark shape against the shiny material around it, still screaming through his nose. His wide, white eyes were visible in the darkness, full of fear and pleading. The plank repeated its motions until the eyes closed shut and the screaming stopped. Gerald stood still, exhausted, arms shaking from exertion. He stared at the boy's still body for minutes, which felt like forever, and dropped the wood to the floor. He crouched down, then got onto all fours, and slowly moved closer to the inanimate child. He could smell the rust now; smell the blood and see its redness, streaked across skin and hair. He thought the boy was dead and was surprised, almost pleased, at how calm he felt. No more stupid things to say now, have you? As the two boys' faces got closer together, it became apparent that he was not dead. He was definitely breathing. He opened his eyes and started to moan again. Calmly, clearly and with no hint of a lie, Gerald said one sentence, "You climbed too high and fell out of a tree, but if you tell anyone anything different, I will kill you."

That night, as he walked home, a pure feeling of happiness filled his stomach. He felt powerful. He was very late home, and was severely punished, but he did not care. Bruises healed and scabs were for picking. In the days that followed, rumours ran wild around the schoolyard. Some were wilder than the truth, but none were precisely correct, so that was the end of it for Gerald. The other boy, however, spent so long away from school in hospital that he had to drop back a year and repeat it. He never once looked at Gerald directly again.

Back in the moment, Gerald thought about the boy and where he might be now. He deserved it, that much was still clear, and looking back on the incident, Gerald smiled. Still smiling, his face now much warmer from the fire, he looked at the contents of the bin. Everything was black, although still burning. Any blood that might still be there would be gone within seconds. A cup of tea beckoned. There was, of course, no functioning electricity for a kettle, but his trusty saucepan on the portable gas stove still did its job. He rarely used it for cooking. He rarely ate much at all, but tea, now that was important. Gerald still smiled, and the grin grew in size as he realised how stupid he had been. He could have just used his mini stove to light the wood. There was no need to have gotten all worked up and angry about the missing lighter fluid. Oh well. It was done now. Problem solved.

The tea was brewing, but the milk smelled vile. No fridge meant no cold storage, even in British weather. The clumpy white mixture poured out onto the grass in lumps like cottage cheese. He poured the black tea from the pan into his Thermos and sat on the bags, reminiscing about more fun times from his childhood.

Chapter 19

As he walked up the gravel path, Jain again decided it was too noisy, so moved onto the grass. He had already confirmed that James Lockedon's car was in a safe position, so a tow truck was not required. It was neither an obstruction nor a safety hazard, and the release fees of removal to a secure yard were ridiculous. He might think Mr Lockedon was selfish for running off, but he did not yet think he deserved that sort of shock upon his return. Reaching the front of the house, knocking the door again seemed a waste of time, so he walked immediately around to the side. As he rounded the east wall of the building he could smell a bonfire. Sure enough, there was the creepy gardener, standing next to a metal bin with flames reflecting in dancing waves across the metallic rim. Jain stood still for a moment and looked at the man ahead of him. He seemed lost in his own thoughts, staring zombie-like at the fire pit. It was like Homo Erectus discovering fire for the first time and being amazed by the sight. Gerald did have a sort of stone-age-man look about him. Intrigued, he moved back to the corner, and stood watching. After a minute, Gerald seemed to snap out of his trance and moved into the shed nearby. Then, he came back out, holding a Thermos and a carton of milk and poured the milk all over the grass, clearly in disgust. Once the carton had then been thrown into the still flaming bin, Mr Stone-age went back into his wooden cave, holding his tea.

"What are you burning?" said Jain, now standing in the shed's doorway without any prior introduction. Gerald's eyes flicked up, still holding the rim of a plastic cup in his mouth. A second passed whilst he looked frozen in shock.

"What do you want?"

"I've got some more questions about that missing person. What are you burning?"

"Just garden waste. What questions? I don't know your missing friend. I already told you."

"Yes, true, but I wasn't as thorough as I should have been. I really need to note everything down properly. Go into a bit more detail. Make sure I've crossed and dotted everything."

Gerald exhaled, steam escaping his mouth. He was clearly unhappy with the detective's presence.

"I know I already asked you some questions, but I do need to be more thorough. The man's still missing, and I want to make sure I haven't missed anything useful you might be able to tell me. So, when did you first notice the car parked out on the road in front of the house?"

"What car?"

"You were out looking at my car yesterday. There's another one further along. It's still there now. Don't tell me you haven't noticed it."

Gerald frowned, almost imperceptibly, "I haven't."

"Really? And you didn't see any person or persons yesterday in the vicinity of the house at all?"

"No."

"Tell me again about the owners of the house. The Macallisters. I've met them before and they don't seem like the holiday type."

Gerald's frown deepened as he processed this information and did not immediately respond. Jain was about to repeat the question, when the answer finally came.

"Then you don't know them very well. They go on cruises all the time. Sometimes for weeks, sometimes for a month or more. I don't really know where they are or when they'll be back. They definitely didn't see your man."

The detective was frustrated. He had expected to rattle the old gardener a bit more, but his plan was clearly not working. He wondered if there was nothing to gain from this conversation.

"OK. Thanks. But, again, I am going to have to take your details down. I need to record everything properly. It's a formal investigation you see. I apologise for the inconvenience, but can you confirm your name and date of birth please?"

"Gerald Atkinson. two-two-zero-five-one-nine-six-one."

"Twenty-second of May, nineteen-sixty-one, correct?"

"Yes."

"And your home address? Do you live here?"

"No. I told you. I don't have keys for the house."

"So, where do you live?"

"I'm between addresses at the moment. I'm staying with a friend in Bristol."

"And where's that?"

"I don't really want to say. They won't like it if I tell you. They don't like the police."

"Fair enough," replied Jain, keeping his voice light, knowing that this patronising tone was winding up the gardener.

"How do you get here then? There are no other cars that I can see."

"Look. I don't have to tell you anything. You've asked about your man, and I've told you what's what." He put his stained plastic cup down on the floor and stood up. Jain watched him as he rose, noticing how close to hitting a shelf on the wall his head came.

Instinctively, as if guided by his unconscious, the detective turned his head and looked at the other shelf—the one he had seen blood on—and was momentarily confused when he saw nothing on the wall. He opened his mouth to ask about it, then something clicked in his lizard-brain, and he turned around further to look through the shed door. Sticking out from the top of the metal bin was a piece of wood, about six-inches wide, and less than an inch thick. He turned his gaze to the floor, where he had seen the spots of blood yesterday. He saw that they, too, were gone, replaced by scratches and gouged wood. His heart pumped harder as the cogs started to turn. His natural curiosity was screaming at him that something was wrong. There was blood here yesterday. The shelf is missing, burning outside. Someone has tried their best to destroy the spots on the floor. There is an abandoned car on the road. There are no places to hide nearby. It is miles to the nearest home, cafe, cash machine, bus stop or other form of civilisation. There was, Jain decided, a massive problem here.

"Tell me again, what are you burning?"

"I told you," Gerald replied, looking down at the detective now, rather than Jain's preferred position of looking up from a seat as before.

"Garden waste. I'm a gardener. Sometimes we burn stuff."

"Where's the shelf from the wall?"

Gerald paused again, his eyes squinting involuntarily, clearly formulating his response, "It's broken. I put something heavy on it and it broke, so I threw it in the bin."

Jain had to be very careful now. By law, if he suspected the gardener of anything criminal, he needed to caution him before asking anymore questions. However, he had nothing to point to a crime that was not merely circumstantial. Everything the gardener was saying could be true. But, on the flip side, there could be a lot more going on. Instead of speaking to Gerald again, he pulled his police radio out of his pocket.

"Three-one-one-nine to control, over."

The communications department immediately responded:

"Go ahead, but we haven't got you booked on."

"Yeah, sorry about that. I forgot. I'm at Neates House estate on the A369. Could I get a PNC person check please, in company with the subject?"

"Go ahead" the comms operator replied, waiting for the details required to run the subject through the Police National Computer, which held all records for all people arrested, charged, or otherwise on the national database of offenders. Jain passed over everything he had about Gerald: name, date of birth and description. As he waited for a response, he looked the man over. The taller man looked older than his supposed age. He looked, from his face, closer to seventy. He was thin and wiry, but over six-feet tall. His clothes were very worn and his hair was a disgrace. His hands were also both clenched.

"Sierra control to three-one-one-nine, no trace, over."

No trace. That meant no record. Jain had suspected this might be the case, but whether through prejudice, intuition or just plain disbelief, he could not stomach the reality that this man had never been in any sort of trouble in his entire life. Nothing to bring him to the attention of a police officer in the past five decades. He was not having it.

"Show me some ID." He ordered.

"I don't have any."

"You must have something. A bank card, a letter, a bill, birth certificate, something with a name on it."

"Nope."

"Right then. In that case, I'm arresting you."

"No, you're not."

Mouth agape, Jain said, "Sorry?"

"You're not arresting me. I haven't done anything and you've got no evidence."

He might be right, Jain thought, but this situation seemed like total bollocks. The man has done something and he was trying to cover it up. He had no identification to prove who he was or why he was here. A lightbulb pinged on.

"Actually, listen up. I'm arresting you on suspicion of trespass and criminal damage. I don't believe you have permission to be here and you cannot provide me with an address or any form of ID to prove who you are. Therefore, I am arresting you so that I can make further enquiries, interview you, and potentially charge you with the offences. You do not have to say anything, but it may harm your defence if you do not mention, when questioned, something which you later rely on in court. Anything you do say may be given in evidence."

The two men then stared each other. It was Gerald's turn to hold his mouth open. Jain waited for a reaction. He realised that he had no backup, no handcuffs, no body armour, no CS pepper spray, no baton, nothing but hope that the man would agree to come along peacefully. Gerald looked into his eyes silently, clearly weighing up his options. There were very few of them. Unclenching his fists, the taller man regained control of his mouth and began to speak.

"OK then. I guess I'm under arrest. What now, officer?"

Jain felt relief wash over him, but tried not to show it. He maintained his facade and spoke calmly.

"You come with me to the police station. We do an interview and some checks. I think we can sort this all out. If you're compliant, then I won't have to handcuff you. Is there anything you need to bring with you? Have you got a phone, a jacket, or anything? I promise I'll drive you straight back here once all the confusion is cleared up and I won't bother you again." He hoped his confident yet compromising tone was enough to keep the gardener on-side. He knew he was pushing his luck right now with this approach.

Standing to one side, showing the open door, he allowed his prisoner to walk in front, then followed him closely, within an arm's length. Desperately hoping that Gerald would not make a run for it. He was on edge, but trying to maintain his composure. Thinking furiously of how this was going to play out in custody. Maybe he really is innocent of everything. Maybe he's never been in any trouble. Maybe I'm going to end up in court for breaching someone's human rights. Jain's thoughts quickly became less confident, seeing every possible way that this could go wrong. He already started to regret his decision.

Chapter 20

Gerald could not believe the arrogance of this officer. Of course he was not trespassing. He really was the gardener. If the occupants had not died by his hands then they could clear this whole thing up. Unfortunately, they were shrouded in the basement, long since decomposed, and were highly unlikely to come to his rescue. He had to control the impact, do damage limitation, get out on bail, disappear again. That was the only solution right now. He could make a run for it. He would probably get away from the officer; he did not look that fit. But, he knew they had helicopters these days, with cameras and special equipment, not to mention big dogs that could run fast and bite hard.

There was no quick way out of this area and if he got caught running then he would never see freedom again. No, the only thing to do now, was go along with the stupid detective. He knew they would ask for ID at the station, which he would not provide. He knew they would take his photo and do messy fingerprints, but the results would not come back for ages. His fingerprints were already on file, from many years ago, but he knew they could not hold him long enough to match them up. Twenty-four hours. That's what the law said, and that was the maximum. If he could get a lawyer and convince the cops that he was just a gardener and he hadn't seen or done anything, then he'd get let out. Even if it was on bail, he'd be out with enough time to get away for good. Take it easy. Don't do anything rash. Be compliant. Be polite.

He kept repeating these mantras to himself as he walked beside DC Jain. Every few steps, indecision and anxiety crept in, and he thought about running. He held his nerve, though, and walked to the awaiting car. How did he end up in this situation? That stupid, self-pitying, drenched rat who had decided to insert himself into my life, he angrily remembered. That selfish bastard, coming here, snooping around, being a pain. And, now, he was buried in the gardens, not deep enough for trained dogs to miss. Thank God, he had not started running. The dogs would find more than just Gerald hiding in these fields.

Calmly, calmly, play along. Make the detective look paranoid. Make the police let him go. Be polite. Do whatever they say. Don't talk too much. Don't lie more than you have to. Gerald's thoughts were going up and down in emotion, like an ECG after a heart attack. The car door was opened for him, so he remained silent and sat in the back seat. Not looking at the arrogant, Indian cop, he stared at the back of the passenger seat headrest and waited patiently. Heart hammering, face unflinching, he prayed that God still had a plan for him that did not end in prison. His eyes glanced at the back of the officer's head. Not the same God as you, he thought. You probably believe in elephant gods and all kinds of weird stuff. Remaining silent, he kept his ignorance to himself, leaned back and stared at the roof for the rest of the journey.

A long time ago, although he could not remember the exact date, Gerald had taken his first ride in a police car. He had been arrested as a teenager and taken to the police station in an old Panda car. The local community

Bobby had arrested him for stealing, and subsequently kicking the shopkeeper who had chased him. The shopkeeper wanted to press charges for assault, but would not have gotten himself injured if he had not tried to protect some penny sweets. Stupid people, putting their safety at risk for some cheap sugar. He remembered how the officer had told him what a silly boy he had been and crime was not a path he wanted to go down. As if he needed to be told. It was easy for PC Plod, in his cushy job, to lecture a teenager with no decent family, no friends, no education and no desire to conform. At the station, the Bobby had rolled his hands in black ink and pressed his fingers on the paper. It was quite exciting at the time. The interview was held in a dusty office and the policeman smoked the whole way through. At the end, they drove him back to the shop, made him apologise and literally smacked him across the back of the head. It was a cliche by today's standards, but he supposed that's how cliches came to exist. He doubted the police would dare to smack kids on the street today. Not that it really did the kids any good. Nor did being soft, though. Nothing worked if the kids had nothing to lose or no fear to play on. Since then, he had lost count of the amount of times he had been arrested, often by the same local police, until he became an adult and the police stopped being so parental.

As an adult, the police were much less willing to let you go with an apology. They became cruel, sometimes extremely violent. One time, a cop had punched Gerald so hard in the head they had to stop the interview and start again later. He did not blame the officers. They were just stupid and violent, like the criminals they chased. What annoyed Gerald more was the way they would not stop talking. In his mind, an interview should be a question followed by an answer. Not a long rant by a self-righteous pig who then just wanted a yes or no response. They talked too much and did not like it when he said nothing in return. They hit him until he agreed with them. That was how he ended up in prison the first time. Prison was actually ok at first. Clean enough, comfortable enough, and people did not bother you if you sat by yourself and said nothing. Food was bland but free and he did his first few weeks without incident. He was kicked out of the gates one day with a bit of cash and the name of his probation worker, who he subsequently met just once. It was, like everything in life, a waste of time. The last time he was in prison was a different story. A very different experience, a living nightmare, and one he thought he would never be free from. He thought he would live the rest of his life in prison, so once he did get released he knew he never wanted to go back.

Suddenly, the sound of the handbrake being wrenched up broke the silence. The engine was off and his door was being opened. He stepped out of the car, maintaining his calm demeanour, and walked alongside the policeman to a heavy metal door. The door opened and a tall, fat man with a massive bunch of keys invited him in. He was very polite, even offering a cup of tea to the both of them, which the policeman declined.

Sipping the tea, he looked around. This was much more modern than the last police station he had been in.

There were cameras in the ceiling, flat screen monitors on the walls, computers being tapped away on and people walking around carrying mounds of paperwork. After about thirty minutes sat on a cold, hard seat, they called his name and he was taken to a high desk, behind which sat another fat man. This one was a sergeant, he knew, thanks to the display of three stripes on each shoulder. The sergeant looked tired. Everyone looked tired. Looking constantly at a computer screen and keyboard, he asked the arresting officer a question.

"What have you got?"

Jain responded like a robot reciting a speech, "I was investigating a missing person and attended Neates House on the A369. I spoke to this gentleman at the location and noticed blood on a shelf and the floor, which at the time I did not think suspicious. However, upon doing further checks I was unable to ascertain this gentleman's details or confirm his reasoning for being on the estate. No one was at the address to confirm he was lawfully there. He also had no ID and refused to provide any address. When I returned to obtain further details from the gentleman, he continued to be evasive with my questions. I then noticed the blood-stained shelf was missing. I saw that he had put it in a large metal bin in the garden and was burning it. The blood on the floor had also been removed as a result of being scratched out by some sort of tool. I formed the suspicion that the gentleman was not there for a lawful purpose and had no permission to be on the grounds. I also suspected that he, therefore, had no permission to cause damage to the property in terms of burning the wood or scratching the floor. As a result, I arrested him on suspicion of criminal trespass and criminal damage.

The sergeant was furiously typing away.

"Mmm. And, what is the necessity?"

"It was necessary to make the arrest in order to conduct a prompt and effective investigation," still in robot mode, speaking like a teacher, "I need to ascertain the gentleman's name and address accurately, as well as conduct an interview in relation to the offences. I also wanted to prevent any further damage to property."

It all sounded like a speech that the sergeant was not really paying attention to. He probably heard the same words on repeat, every single day. Once the detective had finished his long diatribe, the sergeant looked Gerald in the eyes and asked if he understood why had been arrested.

"Yes. But I haven't actually done anything. I really am the gardener."

"That's what we're going to establish." Sergeant Fatty responded. "I'm authorising your detention for the purposes of a tape-recorded interview, and so the officer can further investigate your involvement in the alleged offences. Whilst you're here you have the right to free and independent legal advice. You can request that advice at any time. If you refuse to do so now, you can change your mind. Would you like to speak to a solicitor?"

"Yes, please."

"I'm also going to authorise the taking of fingerprints and photographs. Any property you have with you will be kept by us and returned to you once you are released from custody. Please sign here." He pointed to a small black rectangle in front of a computer screen. There was a small pen-shaped piece of plastic attached to it on a string. Gerald was confused.

"It's all digital these days," Jain explained. "Use that like a pen and sign on the pad."

Reluctantly, he picked up the stick and scribbled on the plastic rectangle. He saw his scribble on the screen. It looked nothing like an actual signature.

"Thank you," Sergeant Tubby said. "Please remove your shoes and put any property on the desk."

Gerald followed all the instructions exactly as requested, silently repeating his mantra of 'stay calm, be polite' in his head. He repeated his name to the officer and gave an address of a hostel he sometimes stayed at in the past. He denied having any mental health conditions, suicidal thoughts or medical problems. Clearly a lie. He had been diagnosed with numerous things he could not pronounce over the years.

"Right. All done. Now if you'd follow my colleague please." The chubby sergeant pointed to the door.

Turning around, Gerald expected to see DC Jain waiting for him, but he was no longer there. Instead, he was greeted by the other fat man with lots of keys from earlier. He followed the fat man, and was strangely looking forward to being put in a cell. He wanted to lie down. The anxiety had exhausted him and he needed to time to think again. They walked past all the cells and into another corridor. At the end of the corridor was a single open door. As they entered the room, it reminded Gerald of one of those tiny cubicles with a twenty-four hour cash machine inside. The kind he had seen people use at three in the morning to take money out. There was a machine, about the same size as an ATM, but with a larger screen. A keyboard pulled out on a tray, and the table under it was completely glass. The fat key holder started tapping on the keyboard.

"Right, I'm going to take your fingerprints now."

"What's this? Where's all the ink?"

"We don't use ink anymore," laughed the key-swinging fatty. "It's all on computer now. *'Livescan'*. Just follow my instructions."

Gerald's temperature rose and he panicked. Computers did not require time to work like people did. He thought about running again, but there was nowhere to go. The smiling, fat, key-wearing prick took hold of his hand. Frozen, in fear, Gerald prayed to God again. His fingers and palm were methodically pressed against the glass table, and everything started to go fuzzy. Gerald felt sick. This was not the plan. This was not what he wanted to do. He did not want to be here anymore. He closed his eyes and prayed harder. His hands and fingers were manipulated and contorted by the detention officer for a couple of minutes, until both men stood completely still.

"Sarge," shouted the detention officer, loudly into the corridor. "We've got a problem."

Gerald looked at the screen and saw his time-shifted reflection. It was definitely his face, but a lot younger. It was a photograph of a young, incarcerated Gerald, except under the photograph was a different name: his real name.

Chapter 21

Sergeant Allard, DC Jain and a sector inspector, Inspector Baron, stared at the print-out. It was many pages long, with a criminal history dating back to the 1970s. Gerald, as he was formerly known, was now locked in a cell with his head in his hands. He had not moved for nearly half an hour. The police officers were engaged in a serious discussion.

"He needs to be further arrested," Baron told the other two men. "Then he needs to go to straight back to prison. No passing go and no collecting £200. Nice work, Saj."

"Thanks boss. But what about the misper? We need to go back to the house and search it. The bloke's clearly got form for being dangerous. Anything could have happened."

Allard interrupted, "We need to do everything by the book. He's in my custody now, so he's my responsibility. Saj needs to further arrest him, then I can authorise his detention. I don't even know if Merryweather Prison is still open. Call a solicitor and interview him. Authorise a search at the premises if you want, but record it on the custody record and get the paperwork ready for court. Let them decide where to send him. I've never dealt with a breach of licence as old as this before. The next court isn't until tomorrow morning, so there's a bit of time."

The men fell silent. Bureaucratic headaches started setting in. It turned out that Gerald the gardener was actually Gilbert Winter: fugitive, child murderer and sex offender. According to PNC, he was last seen in 1998 by his probation officer, whilst released into the community on licence. He had not signed on and kept appointments as required, so the courts issued a warrant recalling him to prison, but by the time they tried to enforce it, he was gone. Technically, he had now been living *unlawfully at large* for over twenty years. Impressive in some ways, worrying in others, but now a problem in Jain's lap. He needed to plan his next steps carefully. He needed advice.

"Can you authorise a search, sir?"

Baron nodded slowly, "Since he's been arrested already, I can authorise a section eighteen, but we need something to look for. There has to be a purpose."

"How about a missing person?" Jain said, less a question, more stating the obvious.

"Unfortunately, that's not what he's been arrested for, so I can't authorise a search for something unrelated to his arrest. We'll get done for going on a fishing trip and anything we find could be thrown out. How about evidence related to the criminal damage? If we're searching for more tools, then they're small enough to justify searching the whole house. It's a bit thin, but technically lawful. I'll authorise it directly onto the custody record and give the paperwork to the search team."

Jain frowned as he asked the next question.

"There must still be evidence of the blood on the floor. Can we ask CSI to go and swab it?"

"Yes, I suppose so, but they need to be looking for something to do with the damage. There's no lawful reason at this stage they'd be looking for blood. If they look for tool marks but find some blood they will obviously need to bag and tag it. That's the way to get it. We've got to be careful how we record and justify our actions. Anything untoward and lawyers will jump on it. I'll speak to whoever's on duty. You get an interview plan together and wait for the solicitor." Baron turned to the sergeant's computer and started typing. Sergeant Allard and Jain started to walk down the corridor towards the cells.

As the heavy, metal door creaked open, Winter—the murderer formerly known as Gerald—was still sat on the solid bed with his head in his hands. He did not look up at his visitors. Jain cleared his throat and began to talk.

"Gilbert Winter, you remain under arrest, however, I am further arresting you for breaching your licence conditions and you will be returned to prison. In the meantime, you're still under caution. You will still be interviewed. A solicitor is on the way. Do you understand?"

No movement from Winter to acknowledge what was happening. The officers looked at each other.

"Mr Winter, do you understand what was said? Do you have any questions?"

No response.

Allard's face was stoic as he spoke, "I'm satisfied that the officer explained himself and I'm satisfied that you understand the process, so I am further authorising your detention so that you can be placed before the next available court."

No response. Gilbert Winter remained still, head bowed, hands over his eyes and forehead. The two officers left the cell and closed the door behind them. As they walked back up the custody office, the detention officer informed them that Gilbert Winter's solicitor was waiting outside. Jain asked for him to be brought through to a private office and went in to sit down. Just moments later, the door to the office opened and the him was actually a her. A well-dressed woman entered. She was short, around five feet two inches tall, slim, with short, blonde hair and red, plastic, clearly fashionable glasses. She immediately started to speak.

"I'm the duty solicitor on call, Helen Talbot, I need a copy of his custody record, PNC print out and any statements you've got, please, officer..."

"Jain. Detective Constable Sajid Jain. I've got the printouts already for you, but there aren't any statements yet. Just my pocket notebook."

She looked over the papers as she sat in the crummy plastic chair. Jain noticed she had red, high-heeled shoes, matching the colour of her glasses. He thought she was attractive, but she was also a solicitor so he already did not trust her at all. Her job was to do anything to get this murderer released and to find fault with the police, no matter how genuine a mistake. Her eyes peered through her glasses, flicking quickly over the printed jargon.

"Are you ready to interview?" She asked.

"Pretty much. There's not a lot to ask at this stage, however, you should be aware that officers are doing a section-eighteen search of Neates House at the moment, so more may come up later. A second interview may be required if you're happy to do a preliminary one now."

"I'll speak to my client first and let you know."

Jain nodded and stood up. He knew this game. They had little evidence of a crime, except his recall, to put to him, and they might end up with more later. He knew exactly how this interview would go, and was willing to bet a thousand pounds that it would be 'no comment' all the way.

The detention officer, Blake, walked Winter up to see the solicitor. It was some form of movement from the murderer at least. He sat in the office with the attractive woman as Blake closed the door behind him. The police officers and police staff were all sat in the sergeant's office drinking tea and talking about how someone could disappear from existence for such a long time. Jain was the quietest, only speaking when questioned, otherwise thinking about the misper's girlfriend. He did not really have an update for her. The boyfriend was still missing, and it was only a hunch that Winter was involved. If he told her that now, and it turned out to be false, it would only cause greater harm. All things considered, and with today's events in mind, he really could not think of anywhere else James Lockedon could be. Short of building himself a tree house in the grounds and hiding from everyone, it only made sense that he had somehow gotten involved with Winter and ended up on the wrong end of a burnt shelf. As he pondered that thought, he was interrupted to be told that they were ready for interview.

Jain's suspicion of a 'no comment' interview grew even stronger after such a short consultation. He took his papers, tea and blank tapes up the corridor to the interview and got ready to start.

The tapes were placed in the machine, but it had not yet started to record as Winter and his solicitor took their seats. No one made eye contact with anyone else. They all knew they were just going through the motions. Complying with the law, whilst being party to its ineffectiveness. Jain pressed the record button and waited for the long, shrill, buzz to stop, indicating the interview had begun.

"I am DC Sajid Jain, 3119 of Tyntesfield Police Station. There are no other officers present. Can you confirm your name for the tape please?"

No response was forthcoming, so he looked at the solicitor. She obliged.

"My client does not wish to speak at this time. I can confirm his name and date of birth, Gilbert Winter, twenty-second of May, nineteen-sixty-one, as recently recorded on the custody record update."

Jain continued, duty bound to do so.

"You have been arrested on suspicion of trespass and criminal damage, namely trespassing on the grounds of Neates House, A369, and causing damage to a shed therein. You have been further arrested for breach of licence dating back to nineteen-ninety-eight. I must advise you that you remain under caution and you are entitled to free and independent legal advice. Do you feel that you have had sufficient time to consult with your solicitor?"

No response.

"My client will not answer any questions."

"Can you explain to me your understanding of the caution?"

No response.

"My client will not answer any questions."

"You do not have to say anything. That means you can remain entirely silent throughout the process and it is your right to do so. You are under no legal obligation to speak. It may harm your defence if you do not mention, when questioned, something which you later rely on in court. That means if I ask you a question today about the offences for which you have been arrested, and you fail to answer them, but the same or similar questions are asked at court, and you do answer them, then the courts may draw an inference from that and wonder why you did not take the opportunity to answer those questions here today. Anything you do say may be given in evidence. That means that anything you say is being tape-recorded or written down and can be presented to the court as evidence related to the offences. That evidence can be both in your favour, or against it. That's what the caution means. Do you understand?"

No response.

"My client will not answer any questions."

"Then I shall begin my questions. Tell me about your actions at Neates House between yesterday and today. Specifically, tell me about why you were there and what you have been doing there."

No response.

"My client will not answer any questions."

Jain continued, "Do you have permission from the owners or other interested parties to be present on the grounds of Neates House?"

No response.

"My client will not answer any questions."

"Do you have permission from the owners or other interested parties to damage any property in, on, or connected to the grounds of Neates House?"

No response.

"My client will not answer any questions."

"Do you have access to the main house?"

No response.

"My client will not answer any questions."

"How long have you been working, living or attending Neates House?"

No response.

"My client will not answer any questions."

"Did you see any people at Neates House yesterday?"

No response.

"My client will not answer any questions."

"Do you know James Lockedon?"

"Officer Jain. My client has not been arrested for any offences relating to an individual by that name, so please refrain from asking about them."

"Is James Lockedon inside the house?"

No response.

"My client will not answer any questions and you should not be asking about anything not related to his arrest, as you specifically alluded when you clearly explained the caution. If you continue, I will terminate the interview."

"It's not your interview to terminate." Jain said, staring at the woman opposite.

"I beg your pardon?"

"It's my interview. I need to ask questions. If Mr Winter feels uncomfortable, he can stop the interview. It's not up to you, so I'd appreciate it if you stopped talking. You have no authority here, so stop acting like you do."

"Right, that's it. This interview is over." She stood up. Gilbert Winter remained seated. The tapes continued to record. He was looking at Jain now. The tension was palpable. Winter looked as though he was about to speak. Instead, he stood up also, and walked to the door.

"OK. I am terminating the interview. The time by the clock in the interview room is two-forty pm." He clicked stop on the tapes.

"How dare you speak to me like that." The solicitor said, clearly furious.

"It's the truth. Know your job. Wait here whilst I take Mr Winter back to his cell. You're not permitted in that area. You might want to stay close by though. I suspect there will be more questions later." He walked off, gripping Winters' arm, before she could start to object.

Chapter 22

A large, white van pulled up to the gates of Neates House. Out of the side doors stepped four large, white police officers. Most officers in the PSU—Police Support Unit—tended to be large and white. It was like an old boys' club. The van's driver, Sergeant Fraser, was also large and white. He was also getting on a bit in years. An old, white man, leading a team of police officers. Just as it always seemed to be. Nevertheless, this team of officers were highly trained in search tactics and had no issues using their large bulk to open doors that people wanted to keep closed. They all cared very little about being stereotyped.

One of the officers carried a black rucksack of tools, whilst another carried the Big Red Key. The Big Red Key was actually a sort of battering ram. Solid metal, bright red and extremely heavy, it was used for opening doors by force, hence its monicker. The officers cut open the padlock, rather unnecessarily, and pushed back the gate before marching up the gravel pathway. None of them were entirely sure what they were being sent to look for, but they were told to search the whole house and any adjoining buildings, so that was what they intended to do, no matter how long it took. To be fair to the team, they were usually swift and efficient, and today would be no different.

Sergeant Fraser knocked on the front door as loudly as possible. He expected, and received, no response. Being a large, thick, wooden door, he beckoned his team to the rear of the building and they walked with him without comment. An efficient unit of muscle, following orders, questioning nothing. As their heavy Magnum boots crunched over the gravel, another set of boots made their way up the path. These boots were much smaller and made far less noise. They belonged to CSI Frost, a slim woman from headquarters who had been sent to find blood, but had written on her documents that she was looking for tool marks. So far, so normal. She quickly caught up with the PSU team and followed them to the rear of the house. As the team of men stopped at the back door, leading into the kitchen, she walked away from them to her target, the shed and immediately got to work.

Frost inspected the tool marks on the floor where she had been informed blood once lay and removed tape from her bag. She began to use the tape to pick up fragments of wood and any other debris that might be hard for the eye to see. A minute into this fiddly task she heard three loud bangs followed by a clang. That will be the back door getting the Big Red Key treatment, she thought to herself. She had once tried to pick up the Big Red Key, and even with both hands she could barely lift it. The other burly officers had laughed at her. She enjoyed that. She was a natural flirt. She enjoyed the men in their tight, black t-shirts, under-sized sleeves, with over-sized muscles. Smiling, she picked up a small, white bottle of liquid to spray on the floor, along with cotton-tipped swabs. As she sprayed, delicately in small areas, she swabbed the residue. Slowly but surely, some of the swabs picked up the telltale red of blood. It was small, but it was there, and you never needed much to run a basic test. The tool marks themselves were a bust. It was impossible from the way they were done to give any indication as to what tool caused them. Not that it really mattered in this case.

She stood up with a groan, and started to take photographs of the area on the floor, followed by the shed as a whole. The courts loved photos. Even when they gave a fraction of the information contained in her reports, it was always the photos that juries spent hours looking at. If she told the jury what they were supposed to be looking at in her photos, then that was almost always what they decided they saw. Humans are so easy to manipulate, she thought. Thankfully, Frost was a professional and only ever reported her findings accurately, but she knew how other officers twisted their words to fit whatever case they were trying to build. Satisfied that she had what she needed, she gave the shabby shed one final look, then zipped everything into her bag and started on the paperwork.

Inside the kitchen and adjacent hallway, a far less delicate operation was in progress. Every cupboard door was open and every drawer pulled all the way out. The team of muscular men opened old jars from the now mouldy fridge, and checked their contents, even if they did not really know why. Nothing was given a free pass and nothing was put back in its place. Within minutes, the kitchen looked as though it had been the scene of a riot, but nothing useful was discovered. Officers individually agreed to go to different rooms, all on the ground floor. If anything of note was discovered, the officer was to shout 'stop' and everyone stopped still until the sergeant gave the ok to continue. This was how things were done by his unit. Often, when police officers searched a property, they acted as individuals and the left hand never knew what the right hand was doing. This too frequently resulted in mixed-up timelines, inconsistent labelling and weak chains of evidence. Not in Fraser's team. There would be no arguments in court about who found what, where and when. Their statements would be consistent and their unity never in doubt. Mistakes were covered up if necessary. What the courts were told was more important than the truth to him. If it looked better for a square to be found before a triangle, then that is how the reports were written. Everyone's statement reflected the same timeline, the same locations, the same words, changed in small ways to look unique, but otherwise factually inseparable.

It was not that Fraser was corrupt. He had never planted evidence. It was simply that he knew, as well as any experienced cop, that the slightest inconsistency was seized upon. Humans were fallible, and even with the best of intentions, they interpreted things differently. This meant that, left to their own devices, a team of officers would report an identical situation differently. That was human. He did not allow human error. He controlled the story that ended up in juror's heads. It was the only way to lock up the criminals he knew needed locking up. And, boy, did more of them need locking up. He was damn sure of that.

An hour passed and the house was trashed. Not damaged or destroyed physically, but it was like Neates House was a full-sized countryside snow globe that had been shaken by a toddler. Piles of the house's once-organised contents were strewn around each room. Clothes were in bundles on the floor and chairs were stacked-up against the walls. Fraser walked the length of the ground floor, inspecting each room. The officers stood still in their respective domain, waiting for the order to move upstairs. Nothing had yet been seized as evidence, and, unsurprisingly, no bodies had been found in jacket pockets.

The last room to be checked on the ground floor was not actually a room, but a triangular cupboard under the stairs. Its three-sided door was open and Fraser could see inside. It was quite big. As wide as the staircase and almost as long. Starting at around six feet high and descending down into a corner. It was carpeted in a dirty old rug, not in keeping with the lovely wooden floors across the rest of the house. He walked inside, bending down further as the ceiling sank under the steps. An old 'Henry' vacuum cleaner, shoe boxes, broken, brass light fittings and dust. A lot of dust. As he walked over the rug, he could feel the floor bend under his weight. This, to him, was a telltale sign. The floor was also a door. A hatch to a basement. He called one of his colleagues over, and between the two of them, pulled out the junk and ripped out the rug. As expected, there was a square-shaped trapdoor underneath.

"Time?" He called out.

"four eighteen," came the reply.

"Note it down," Fraser commanded as he pulled back the latch and lifted the panel. It opened to the side and was easily propped up against the wall. Wooden steps were permanently in place leading down to the dark basement. He carefully placed his right boot on the top step, slowly adding more of his weight to test the stability of the wood. He had fallen through steps before and was not the owner of self-deprecating humour. Confident that the steps were sturdy, he walked down them slowly, carefully testing each one. It was almost pitch-black so he slid the foot-long metal torch from his belt and clicked it on. The basement was immediately flooded in light. It looked like most other basements. The walls were unpainted plaster, the floor was uncovered concrete, and there was the usual junk and sheet-covered boxes one often saw in forgotten storage. The second officer, co-rug-puller, followed Fraser down the steps and looked at the sergeant, awaiting instructions.

"Have a quick look, but don't break anything," came the order. The officer complied and started pulling off sheets creating a cloud of dust reflecting the torchlight. Cardboard boxes full of bedding and clothes, as musty as a nursing home, filled each one. Finally, in the corner against the far wall was the shape of an old rolled up carpet, covered in another white bedsheet. It was not white anymore though. It had turned a stale, tobacco yellow, with a side order of thick, grey dust. He peeled it back, slowly and carefully, trying his best not to create even more clouds to breathe in.

As the sheet peeled free of its contents, he muttered, "Fucking hell."

Fraser agreed. "Fucking hell. Call Frost down here."

CSI Frost stepped carefully down into the basement, trying her best not to touch the grim surroundings for support. She saw the whole PSU team stood in the large room and took in her surroundings. Dust: check. Boxes: check. Junk: check. Dead bodies: check?

Two decomposed adult-human-sized corpses lay on their backs against the far wall. Lying together like an old couple in their marital bed, only this bed was a set of dirty, stained sheets on a concrete mattress. Not very romantic. The bodies no longer had the stench of death, thankfully, as they had long since liquefied and leaked into their surrounding materials. All that remained were dry, skeletal shapes. Not white, like skeletons in movies. These still had the brown-grey-black shading on the surface, resulting from oxidisation of iron in the now-absent blood. Insect damage seemed minimal, but that was hard to tell now that their potential food source had long-since dried out. How much had naturally decomposed and how much had been consumed by parasites was debatable. Only the two heads were fully visible, due to the rest of their bodies being covered by numerous layers of bedding. Being the most exposed, she assumed the heads would display the greatest level of decomposition. Teeth had fallen out of place and the eye sockets were empty. Some hair still remained, however, thin and brittle on the top. The body cavities inside may give more clues as to the cause of their demise. It took a bit longer for internal organs to decompose if the body was well covered. However, this room was warm and dry.

Skeletonisation was well underway, so internal organs were likely to be completely devoid of moisture by now. She was not a pathologist or a medical scientist, so could offer no guess as to how long they had been there. Many months, at least, possibly years, she guessed.

She had seen many dead people in her time on the job, but never as creepy as this. She had been to fresh murder scenes, red rooms spray-painted in arterial blood, hangings, suffocations, car crash decapitations and most other forms of death. However, this was just chilling. It reminded her of the fruit cellar from 'Psycho' and Norman Bates' mother, although these victims were not sat in a chair. It conjured images of a twisted taxidermist keeping his trophies in a secret, personal museum. They almost certainly did not get there by themselves.

She started taking photographs of everything in situ. Evidentially, there would be little to find, but a team would need to come in and work the area. She took as many pictures as she thought necessary before everything got moved out of place by her friends in white masks.

"Everybody needs to move out of the room," she said, confidently. "Get a scene log going and inform the inspector. We're going to be here a while."

Chapter 23

Inspector Baron listened carefully to whoever was on the phone. His face twisted in a mix of disgust and concentration. He gave the occasional affirmation to the caller, but little else. Eventually, he hung up without saying goodbye.

"Jain," he called. The detective was checking his emails at a desk nearby.

"Listen up. PSU and CSI are at the house. They've done searches. The CSI found the blood you talked about. Not much, but there are swabs. She's getting them looked at now. PSU searched the basement and found two bodies. They're not your misper though. These bodies have been there a hell of a lot longer than a day or two. There's a CSI team and supervisor attending to deal with that. It looks like Winter might need to be arrested again, this time for a double murder. Voters roll shows two names at the address. Mr and Mrs Macallister, an elderly couple, so there's a high chance that's who the bodies belong to. This is getting out of hand. I need you to liaise with a CSI called Frost. She took the swabs and is getting them checked. If the misper's dna isn't already on file, we'll need something to compare her samples against."

"He is, boss." Interrupted Jain. He had it taken from an arrest for public order years ago. Some drunken incident with a few people in Bristol. He wasn't convicted, but the samples are still on file, along with his fingerprints."

"Right. Well, triple-check they weren't purged. We're not supposed to keep samples of people that aren't convicted. I know we do, but we had still better check. Frost can probably do that for you. Try and find out if the Macallisters could be anywhere else, or if there's any family to contact. I need to see the Chief Inspector upstairs, so keep your phone with you and make sure it's on loud."

Jain nodded as Baron walked past him looking mightily stressed. He could not really be blamed. This was a nightmare, not just on a human level, but bureaucratically. There was very little chance of anyone going home on time. He suddenly felt bad for that thought. It was not as if there was anything waiting for him at home to go to. The overtime was nice and this was a good case for his promotion prospects. Sadly, that was how he needed to think. To attribute human emotion to death and murder was too depressing to comprehend.

Winter had a lot more questions to answer now. First, though, was the matter of CSI. He really wanted to know if his suspicions were correct, and that the blood on the floor was Lockedon's. If it was, and he was getting more sure about that, then where was the man? Maybe— hopefully—it was an injury that he had walked away from. That created its own problems, but regardless of Jain's professional motivations, he really did not want to find out the man had been murdered. He could not face breaking that news to the parents. They were lovely, if a little over the top. The mother, in particular, was devastated when he had been missing for less than a day. Goodness knows how they felt now. They would almost definitely be totally destroyed if their son was gone for good. And the girlfriend. Shit. If the records had been purged, he might need to get something from her with Lockedon's DNA. A toothbrush, comb, dirty clothes or something similar. That created more questions than he wanted to answer.

Driving over to HQ took about thirty minutes from the custody unit. HQ was where all the CSI, training, senior leadership and external departments were based. Face-to-face discussion was a lot better than a phone conversation, so he wanted to see Frost in person. Plus, other CSI's and admin staff would be there to follow up on anything he needed. Ironically, the journey from custody to HQ was quicker by taking the A369. The irony of that was not lost on him, and as he approached Neates House he caught sight of the white cars and vans parked near the main gate.

Staff in paper suits were huddled by one of them, probably discussing their morbid task. He refocused on the road and took the bend too fast. He had a sudden surge of adrenalin as he realised he was driving too quickly. Luckily, nothing was oncoming, but he needed to calm down. Jain was like a swan: on the surface he gave the appearance of calmness and serenity, but underneath he was paddling like a madman thinking a hundred thoughts at once. The magnitude of this case was starting to hit him. What started as a very simple, common or garden missing person job had escalated into a probable double murder. Triple-murder, potentially, if his worst nightmares came true. The severity of any mistake from this point was massive. He felt out of his depth. He knew that senior officers were taking the lead and making the decisions, but this had all been driven by him. His instincts had lead to

Winter's arrest: a fugitive, convicted murder, at-large for years, now a suspect in a probable new murder, and linked to a now high-risk missing person. It was so sudden, yet would have been inconceivable just two days ago.

Finding a parking space in the huge HQ car park was surprisingly difficult. It seemed as though more police staff worked in cushy office jobs than were actually out on the streets. Politicians would have a field day if they knew what most of the public budget was really spent on. The public, already cynical, would blow a gasket if they could see the number of cars parked here; especially when many in the public had been waiting a day or more for a police officer to show up. He found a space near the gymnasium, another excess, and walked into the main building.

CSI commandeered a large area within headquarters, rightly so. Their offices were not much like their TV counterparts, but it was still impressively technological. He spoke to the receptionist and asked to see CSI Frost. The girl behind the desk put her mobile phone down on the desk as he spoke. The Facebook app was open on the screen. She advised him that Frost was in with the FSS. The FSS was the Forensic Science Service, who used to be entirely external. Samples took weeks to be tested and cost a fortune. In 2012, a few years after reputational damage (from botching some work on a case involving a young murder victim named Damilola Taylor), they closed their doors, but their research methods were retained by the government. As a result, individual consultancies were created across the country, and some forces subsidised their testing by paying for on-site staff to work for them directly, technically independent of the police. The 'new' FSS was incredible in its scope. Decades-old crimes were being solved thanks to their expertise on tiny pieces of ageing materials. Being on-site meant that now, in extreme circumstances, tests for DNA could be rushed through in-house rather than sent to slow, expensive, external labs. This case, he believed, was pretty extreme. It was worth the expense.

Frost could see him walking to the door, and although they had never previously met, intuition on both sides made it clear who each person was. She beckoned him in.

"I gave the blood swabs directly to FSS about an hour ago. It will still take hours to get a match. Lockedon's sample is in our system, so it will be a direct comparison. They're not testing for anything in the blood itself, though, so if he was drugged or under the influence of something, we'll need to do other tests for that."

"I just want to know if it's his," Jain muttered.

"Well, that's the plan. If it is his, then we can tell you this evening. Anything else will take longer as we'll need to run new tests, and we don't have a huge sample to play with, so only certain tests can be done. Let's hope it didn't come from someone that isn't on our systems or we'll be in the poop."

Her formality and innocent language seemed quite cute, even in the midst of something so serious. When everybody else was dropping F-bombs and acting like their heads were about to pop, her knowledgable professionalism was calming.

"Thank you," Jain said, meaning her demeanour rather than her work, but she was oblivious to his sentiment.

"Are you going to stay and wait?" She asked.

"I'm staying around here, but I do need a phone and a computer."

"You can use my desk. It's over there, nearest the clock. The one with the photo frames."

As he approached the desk and sat down, he looked at the photos. Three smiling children were looking at the camera. He presumed the children were hers, all under ten, and felt a pang of disappointment. He was not going to be so unprofessional as to ask her out on a date, but the sudden realisation that such an opportunity was unlikely still scratched at his masculine ego. He really needed to stop seeing every woman as a potential date. He was not looking for a girlfriend, but the fact he kept thinking like this was probably an unconscious signal. He did not think he was lonely, but any reasonable person looking from outside would assume that he was. Maybe they were right. He had just met someone in the past few minutes and was disappointed that they were already taken. At least, he assumed she was. Shaking the thoughts aside, he picked up the phone and dialled. A deep voice answered.

"Yeah. Go ahead."

"Hi Mark, it's Saj."

"Alright mate. How's it going."

"It's going," said Jain, his usual neutral response. No wonder he was never invited anywhere. "You might have heard. We just found two bodies up near the A369. I was hoping you were free for an area search with your partner?"

"Can be. I'm down near Taunton at the minute. By 'bodies' do you mean murder?"

"Yeah. Historic. They've been there a while, but there is a third-party that's missing. We found blood at the scene and there's a good chance it belongs to the misper. I want to know if there's any other sign of him on the estate," explained Jain.

Mark Vivian was a Police Constable in the PSU unit, like the team that searched the house earlier, but was also linked to both the traffic department and the dog section. Basically, he travelled around huge areas of the south west of England with his scary-looking German shepherd until he was called to a job. Anything went for the dog handlers: crowd control, searches for people or evidence, or any situation where the presence of a well-trained dog might help.

"I'm on it mate. Get comms to send me the details and I'll head straight up. Probably an hour or so."

"Thanks. I'll let them know." Jain hung up the phone and dialled the communications department, who were only across the corridor. It seemed silly to phone them when they were so close, but their entire jobs revolved around wearing headsets and talking to faceless recipients. Talking to them in person might spin their tiny minds. He passed over details of the dog handler and asked them to put him into the incident on their system. He leaned back in the chair and looked up at the ceiling. What now? He thought. Was everything being done that could be done? What was he missing? He hated waiting and now, it seemed, that was all he could do.

Chapter 24

Claire was at James' parents' house in Winscombe, a small village outside Weston-super-Mare. They were all sitting in the lounge nursing cups of tea, talking about James. Every sentence seemed to have an air of hope to it, as if to discuss the worst was going to make it true. Claire looked at the two of them, sat close together on the chunky, cream sofa. They seemed to have aged overnight. John Lockedon had once been in the army. He was usually very quiet but always well-presented. Today, he had stubble on his cheeks, and looked understandably agitated. Mairi, James' mother, was usually smiling. She rarely sat down, being always busy making cups of tea or offering biscuits. Today, she too looked forlorn and lethargic. They had probably not slept much. Claire was also feeling drained. She had heard nothing from the police to suggest they were doing anything to find James, and her calls had not yet been returned. She felt helpless. More accurately, she felt angry and useless; she wanted to do more.

Suddenly, her phone rang. Everyone looked at it, buzzing on the coffee table, not even trying to hide their desperation that it was James calling. They would forgive him for anything at this moment: some impromptu vacation that he had not told anyone about, or a trip to a rehab centre for an undisclosed drug addiction—anything that meant he was safe and well. Their worries were not allayed. Claire answered, listening intently to the voice with the unknown number.

"Hello, DC Jain," she said, looking at the two beleaguered parents. Their eyes were fixed on Claire, wider than normal with a hopefulness that was heartbreaking.

"No. We haven't heard from him."

The two retirees' eyes dropped. Such a simple sentence that meant their world was still in tatters. They both looked into their cups, perhaps hoping for a message in the tea leaves. Generally sensible people, they would believe anyone right now if it was a message of hope. If a TV psychic knocked on the door proclaiming to be in metaphysical contact with James, they would force themselves to believe it. They would give their lives' savings for a message of his safety. Their son was still their baby. Mairi, especially, had never stopped looking at him in that way. All grown-up with a proper job and his own flat, he was still someone she wanted to take care of. She often offered to do his laundry or give him money, but he always refused. He rarely visited, and when he did he barely spoke. Claire was always the one doing the talking.

James had seemed indifferent to his parents, but Claire was always lovely. Mairi wondered if she had done something wrong. Maybe she had been a bad mother and he had decided to run away. She could not understand why he always seemed so negative about everything. Every time she suggested that he be more sociable or get a hobby, he replied with, "what's the point?". John told her that he was just a typical man who did not want to share his feelings. "He's still a bit of a lad," John would say. He once told her to stop worrying. "He'll be happier when he finds the right girl and settles down with a family." Claire, they believed, was definitely the right girl for James. They could see how happy she was with him. Always touching his hand, looking at him with a smile. Mairi knew Claire wanted children, but hoped they would get married first. She was old-fashioned like that. She wanted to be a grandmother, but more importantly, she wanted James to come back.

Claire put the phone down.

"That was the police. They haven't found James yet. They're still investigating. He said they found some evidence that James might have been at that big house I told you about, but that they were still looking into it, following leads or whatever."

Neither parent spoke at first. Eventually, Mairi gave a small cough.

"Thanks Claire. You're such a comfort. I'm sure it'll be alright in the end. By God, that boy's in trouble when he comes home. He's not too big for a smacked bottom!" She joked, failing to raise a smile.

Chapter 25

Gilbert was lying down now. He felt a moment of calm. His eyes were closed and his hands were clasped together across his chest. That solicitor was good, he thought. Very strong and knowledgable. The police basically had nothing to go on, she told him. Who cared now though? The warrant from the courts was non-negotiable. He was, soon, being returned to prison. There was no appeal, no mitigating factors, no alternative. There was one positive: it turned out that the prison he once resided in was no longer running. He would be sent somewhere new. That was almost a comfort. As much as he did not want to go back to prison, the fact that he would never go back to '*that*' prison was a slight relief. It was that place that he had been running from for all these years. That place that gave him the fear to disappear. He would rather die than go back there, and now he knew that he never would.

The images of that place, those people, the wardens, the inmates, would forever be etched in his mind, but that is where they would stay. Never again would he be forced to look at those walls, and he prayed to the Lord that his punishment was over. For he had been punished. In that place was a punishment that even God could not have ordered. Desperately, he tried to turn his thoughts elsewhere as the memories came flooding back.

Despite keeping himself to himself, Gilbert had been mocked relentlessly from the first day he walked into Merryweather. Every other inmate seemed to be part of a group. Even the other newbies, like him, had aligned themselves within a day. Not Gilbert, though. Nobody liked Gilbert. They knew what he had done and wanted nothing to do with him. He knew what they thought of him, so he stayed near the guards, expecting them to keep him safe. No such luck. They hated him more than the criminals did. Protesting innocence was pointless. That was what 'paedos' and child killers always said. No one would ever believe a word that came out of his mouth. They looked at him with disgust and walked away whenever he approached them.

He managed to survive almost a week before his first beating. He was in the prison library, sat at a desk when he was struck from behind by someone. Three men stood over him, one was holding an encyclopaedia, clearly the weapon of choice in this location. His ears were ringing from the book's heavy contact, so he closed his eyes to try and reorientate. Before he opened them, he was kicked hard in the stomach. The pain was incredible. Not as bad as being burned, but almost enough to make him sick. Then, the three men took it in turns to kick him until a guard came to break it up. He could not stand up properly for days after that.

In the end, his first beating was like a bubble bath compared to what followed. Guards seemed to take longer to come to his rescue. Sometimes, they never came at all. Budget cuts and understaffed, he was told, when he eventually made a complaint. After that, he was a 'grass' as well, so it just got worse. He got used to the beatings, almost drowning out the pain with his mind. Broken bones healed. Bruises faded. It was his new way of life. Eventually, his haters—and there were many of them— decided that their violence was no longer enough. Gilbert could still feel the humiliation of the first time he was raped.

One afternoon, between work detail and dinner, Gilbert was walking back from the yard, past the laundry rooms. He was aware of how few people seemed to be there when he was gripped around the chest in a bear hug. Another person wrapped their arms around his legs, and he was carried into a room full of washing machines. The noise of their drums spinning was as clear today as it was years ago. He was dropped unceremoniously face down onto the floor. One man, the bear hugger, knelt over him with a knee on each side of his head. His arms were twisted up behind his back, and a second man sat on his ankles and feet. Gilbert did not try to struggle. That only ever made things worse. He waited for the kicks and tensed his muscles in anticipation of the pain his ribs would soon feel. Instead, he felt his trousers being pulled over his buttocks. He felt confused. Were they going to spank him, like his father used to? He heard someone undoing their clothes. It sounded like a belt buckle, even though inmates were not allowed belts, and briefly expected to be whipped by it. He waited for the sharp, stinging strikes to cut into his exposed skin. Then, as if struck by new wisdom, he realised what was happening.

He started to shout and wriggled, fought to get free. This was not ok... This was not ok. The knees gripping his head got tighter and he thought his skull might crack.

Then, a new pain that he had never experienced before confused his already over-stimulated brain. A man was on top of him, skin on skin, forcing himself into Gilbert with aggressive thrusts. As his skin tightened and tore, he felt the wetness of blood leak between his legs. He could not stop himself from struggling but knew he could not escape. Eventually, exhausted, he gave up and waited for the end. When it was over, he did not move. Hours later, he was taken to hospital and the police came. They asked for a statement, knowing he would never give one. One day later, he was back in Merryweather, humiliated, unable to look at anyone. Whenever he caught someone's eye they smiled sarcastically, laughed or blew kisses.

From that day, he knew that he had to get out. At first, he tried to kill himself, but he was never left alone long enough, and did not have anything better than bedding to make a rope with. The guards saved him from himself far more quickly than they ever saved him from his tormentors. He asked to see doctors, who referred him to psychiatrists and, ultimately, he was allowed to have more private time away from the inmates. Psychiatrists came and went. Each one diagnosed him with a different set of disorders needing different medications. Those tablets were hard to get once he eventually got out, though. He had not taken any of them in years.

He took courses, read books, and did anything that could be written on his record as a positive. He would be 'rehabilitated', even though he knew such a thing was impossible. If 'rehabilitation' meant freedom, then he would jump through any hoop to get there. A life sentence never meant life. Fifteen years was the time it took for Gilbert to become eligible for early release. He was a model prisoner. Fifteen years of violent rape, stigmatisation and humiliation to keep him motivated. He gave up trying to kill himself and turned to God, who he now knew was putting him on the right path. Once he had redeemed himself in God's eyes, the courts saw that he was no longer a danger. He was ultimately granted early release on licence, and set about his new life. So why, after all these years, had God abandoned him again? Why was he being sent back to a place that allowed such things to happen to him? It was not his fault. He needed help and had gotten it. He was better now. He could not survive another Merryweather. He prayed non-stop for somewhere better. He would be good, he promised.

Chapter 26

Frost approached her desk with a bundle of A4 paper. She held it in her hand as she walked, holding it up like a prize. As she placed it on the desk for the waiting detective to see, she began to explain the jargon printed in black:

"It's definitely James Lockedon's blood. Look here. DNA fingerprinting makes it virtually impossible for this sample to have come from someone else. One in a billion, literally. Your instincts were right, but we still need to find him."

Jain stared at the paper, still sceptical.

"Is it really that accurate? I don't want to mess this up."

"Yes, all we know is that this piece of DNA matches the DNA on record. Nothing more. Assuming that there hasn't been any contamination to either sample, which is unlikely as there was only one person's DNA in the sample we tested. What it doesn't tell us is how it got there, how long it had been there, or where the owner is now. That's still your job."

"That's what I'm trying to find out. I've asked a dog handler to search up at the house. If there's anything human to be found, then they'll find it. It's crazy. This was supposed to be so simple—a standard misper—but now we've got bodies, blood, a fugitive in custody, and the misper is still a misper. I almost hope he's disappeared for good and done a runner to Spain with a stripper or something. The alternative is too grim at the moment."

Frost did not respond to that. There was no question she could answer or advice she could give. Her job was complete. Science gave you answers. She did not believe in silly things like fate, religion or the afterlife. People's emotional decisions and subsequent actions were out of her domain. Although she was curious about the case, she was satisfied that she'd done what she could. She felt a bit sorry for the detective in her chair. He looked confused and worried. Officers were doing their jobs, senior staff were giving orders and he was trying his best to think of ways to get the right result. That was all anyone could ask, she thought. Certain men seemed to have that problem sometimes. A hero complex, rather than a rational acceptance that they could not save every person all the time.

Jain noticed the silence and tried to fill it.

"Anyway, thanks a lot, you've done a great job. I still can't believe it's his. I obviously thought it might be, but wouldn't have bet on it." He stood up from the chair, tucked in his dishevelled shirt and smiled weakly.

"Cheers."

Frost stayed sitting.

"No problem. Just doing my job," she replied. "If you need anything else, give me a buzz on my radio."

"Will do."

With that, he walked back towards the car park deciding what to do next. He had a few options: return to custody and interview Winter before the clock ran out on his detention, wait for the dog handler to come up with something at the scene, or contact the inspector and ask for advice. By the time he started driving, he had decided to go back to the custody unit. That was where he could get the most done.

Arriving at the unit, Jain walked back into the sergeant's office. Allard was still there, tapping away. They exchanged pleasantries, but the sergeant was obviously in the middle of dealing with some other prisoner's problems. As a custody sergeant he was ultimately responsible that everyone detained there was treated properly. Lawful detention, legal advice, human rights, welfare checks, arranging appropriate adults, mental health checks, meals and more. It was more like running the world's worst hotel, but with the threat of prosecution if he made a mistake with the guests in his care. Therefore, he stayed away from the outside actions of officers. He did not want their problems or mistakes rubbing off on him. He gave advice if it was asked for, but was not going to do their job for them.

There was a massive conflict of interest sometimes, between maintaining the rights of a detained person and helping the officers build a case for conviction. Allard believed that one day, his job would not be done by a police officer at all, and that might not be a bad thing.

Jain sat on the other side of the office, deep in thought. He knew that Winter had to be in court tomorrow one way or another. Alternatively, he could be taken straight to a prison, if that was required. Either way, he had to make sure that everything was done properly. The paperwork required paragraphs of text to be filled in, detailing times, people, places, reasons, lawful use of powers, and duplicated across various forms. He might as well get on with that before doing another interview. At the same time, he was hoping Inspector Baron might walk in and offer some help. He did not want to ask for help, as that made him look weak, but if the boss offered it then he would nod along as if that was his original plan. He really needed a body. Or, at least, some indication that Lockedon was still breathing. The lack of knowing this single fact was holding him up and there was precious little time to waste. He felt stressed.

Closing his eyes for a moment, he thought about the chain of events so far. What had he missed? Winter was clearly a murderer. He was also a liar. He had lied about Lockedon being at Neates House. He had lied about his identity. He had tried to destroy evidence of violence. He was keeping two dead, elderly victims in a basement. He had basically stolen their home. He had a history of violent crime dating back to his teens. He had been in prison, trusted with release into the community, then almost immediately disappeared, breaching that trust as well as the law. He was totally fucked. And he deserved to be. All Jain had to do was get him to admit it, tell him where the misper was, and save everyone the hassle and pain of a court case. He opened his eyes, determined to get Winter for everything he deserved, and started making interview notes in preparation for that eventuality.

He had only written the words 'Suspect's Agenda' at the top of his notepad when his radio beeped.

"Yep, go ahead."

"It's Mark. I'm up at Neates House."

Jain tried to keep the sound of desperation out of his voice, almost afraid to ask the inevitable.

"What have you got?"

Chapter 27

PC Mark Vivian was stood at the rear of Neates House, a leash wrapped around his right arm being tugged by a beast with great strength. The house was beautiful, he thought. It must be amazing to live in such peace and quiet. Of course, nothing was more quiet and peaceful than death, and you did not need massive gardens, trees or a mansion to obtain that. He thought about the bodies inside and cringed. He too had seen more death than he ever needed. He once found a body of a heart attack victim, who had fallen mid-cardiac arrest and landed against their electric heater. The contact started a small fire, thanks to the heater's consumption of polyester fibres and cotton undershirt. In the end, all Mark saw at the scene was a human-shaped piece of barbecue, overdone on the back, but still a bit fatty and undercooked on the front. He was grateful for the knowledge that the victim had died before the burning started.

Since then, he had seen every form of human corpse imaginable. That was part of his role in being sent to every kind of job whenever there was evidence or a person to be found. He had become extremely desensitised to the visuals, but still felt empathy for those impacted by the loss of loved ones. He was grateful that his job was mostly physical and that the passing on of difficult news was down to someone else.

This evening, he was looking for fresh meat. Some bloke was missing and had left a spot of blood in the shed. From there, little else was known, so he set about his task with methodical precision. Police dogs were incredibly valuable assets, treated by their handlers with all the love and care they would give a family pet. Sometimes more so. Contrary to popular belief, police dogs did not usually follow your scent, especially when searching outdoors. They were primarily lead by the path you created when you tried to run away. If you ran through a field to escape a chase, the dog could sense your path thanks to the trampled grass and smell of the freshly damaged ground. In other ways, their senses were incredible, picking up on the blood on a knife or hidden firearms ammunition from many metres away. When it came to finding dead bodies, they were incredible. A well-trained dog's olfactory sensitivity allowed them to sense blood in tiny amounts, discriminating it from other smells and careful concealment. If there was a body, or someone bleeding, this dog would find them.

The evening was settling into night. The sun was long gone, but the moon was bright enough to light up the gardens. The trees created ominous shadows across the grass. Their branches like witches' fingers, projecting gothic shadow puppets on a dark green canvas. Mark walked with the dog, leading it—and being lead by it—around the eastern edge of the estate. Their movements looked stilted and random, but were actually precise and methodical. Eventually, they reached a large tree near the north-eastern corner and the dog made its discovery known.

Mark watched his canine partner lie down on the grass next to the tree. He could see a small step-ladder, only three rungs high, folded on its side on the ground. The dog's actions were a passive alert, indicating the presence of some human smell in that spot. Mark assumed that the old gardener had used the step ladder to trim the tree's branches. One of the branches, above the ladder, was bent awkwardly. It was a thick, heavy branch but had a strange bend that seemed unnatural, as though some kids had been playing and pulling on it. It had not been fully snapped or broken, but was also not jutting out the way it should. The officer took a picture with his cellphone of the tree and the ladder in their found positions, and recorded the time in his notebook. He encouraged the dog to stand, gratefully ruffling its fur in appreciation for doing a good job. Praise, not punishment, worked better with animals.

They continued along the perimeter, slowly and carefully. It was really dark in this part of the grounds, but Mark did not want to shine his torch around. He hated the way torches distracted the dog, so relied on the animal to be the leader, taking him along at the right pace. The dog was clearly agitated and had a fixed path that it wanted to take. Mark tried to add restraint to its movements but knew that his furry partner had a determined personality.

Less than twenty metres from the suspicious tree, the dog came to a halt again. This time, the alert was too active. Mark's adrenaline spiked. Sniffing enthusiastically at the ground, walking back and forth over the same spot, the dog had something more than a minor scent of human activity. The dog was excited. Mark encouraged it to lie down, stroking and praising it. If something was here, he did not want it disturbed. The ground was clearly different here. It had not been visible from back at the house or the tree-laden east edge. The soil was freshly dug, dark brown and lumpy. The earlier rain had kept it soft, it seemed. He stood still, not wanting to disturb it either, and unclipped his radio. He called Jain to inform him that he had found something important, and was about to get it uncovered.

Chapter 28

Jain felt a flood of emotion. Anxiety was replaced with excitement. He was gripping the radio so tightly that his knuckles were white.

"Absolutely... Get the Inspector to agree.... PSU are already there.... Just make sure everything is recorded properly. You know what they're like. I need time of discovery, photos. Shit. I'll ask Frost to come back. No. Wait, she's contaminated now with the other blood sample. That means I'm contaminated. Fuck. We need a CSI down there. Someone to record everything. Could it possibly be something else?" He spoke too fast and needed a moment to think. Thankfully, he was interrupted:

"It could be a rabbit warren with fresh, dead animals inside, I suppose. Not likely though. It's a pretty big patch of ground that's been messed with. Obviously by humans, not an animal, in my opinion of course." Mark spoke calmly, sensing his colleague's excitement. He felt it inside too. It was what the job was all about for him.

Jain took over again and carried on rambling at a thousand miles an hour.

"Right. Good. Stay put. Don't touch it, obviously. Sorry, don't mean to patronise. Get a supervisor on it. Get it checked. Thanks mate. Sorry to drop you in it. You'll probably be there a while now."

"No worries bud. It's part of the job. A bit of OT never hurt anyone."

Mark was happy about the OT, overtime, it was going into his rest days, which meant double pay if he could make it last long enough. The fact that this could be a dead body, maybe even a murder victim, with friends and family did not diminish his thoughts of cash. He was, well and truly, desensitised by this job. He cared about doing the right thing, but did not allow himself to put a human emotion on his discoveries. That would be insufferable.

He hung up the call.

Almost immediately, another buzz came through on Jain's radio: Inspector Baron.

"Jain?" Asked the crackling voice.

"Yes, sir, go ahead."

"I guess you've heard the update. I've asked for further officers to come and do scene preservation. We've had to call in other sectors to help. A CSI is up with PC Vivian at the new scene, and they will take photos and do their usual business before having a look. There's no point guarding a buried pet, if that's what it turns out to be. Although, the dogs are pretty good and if it's looking for a human then I'm sure it's found something human. Anyway, stand by. Once we know what it is, I'll update you and you can re-interview Winter. Either way, we can't wait much longer before interviewing him again. I've asked DS Manos to assist you with that. She's on her way over. She knows what she's doing. I'll get back to you both when I know more from here."

The transmission ended abruptly and left Jain under no illusions. He would definitely bet money on that 'disturbed ground' being Lockedon. Nothing else made sense. He hoped that he was not the one tasked with telling the parents. He could not face that today. Please be wrong. Please be a dead cat or something, he silently wished.

There was nothing else he could do at this moment but sit and plan the interview. He was not entirely happy that this other person, DS Manos, was being sent over, but he knew it made sense. This was no longer just a bit of criminal damage and suspicious behaviour. It was suspected murder, and one with some holes in their knowledge of the story. If they had witnesses, things would be easier, but there was nothing but circumstantial evidence tying Winter to any crimes on the estate, maybe excepting the damaged shelf. The custody sergeant's office suddenly felt very small. He needed space. He needed a desk to really plan things out properly and he needed a bit of respite from the prisoners constantly banging their doors or shouting for phone calls and cups of tea.

He picked up what paperwork he had already accrued, thanked Allard and walked out of the custody suite entirely. He trudged upstairs to the CID offices, hoping everyone had gone home. The stairs in this station matched everything else about it: worn, dusty and in need of an update. His footsteps caused the floor to creak. He suddenly felt tired again. The rush of adrenaline and short-term excitement had worn off. His body craved a new boost of energy. Unfortunately, there were no canteens or caterers here, unliked at headquarters. He briefly considered going out to get food but could not face the thought of eating. What his body needed and what his mind wanted were two different things right now.

The CID office was, indeed, empty. No-one in these departments worked late unless they were on call or on the late roster. Jain was the late roster CID this week for the area, so he had the room to himself. At least, until DS Manos turned up. He wondered what sector she covered, not recognising the name.

He found the largest, clearest desk and set himself up. Computer on, lights on, paperwork in piles, it already looked more promising. Laying out his barely-started interview plan, he started adding key points to it. He recreated the timeline of events, as he saw them, in notes across the page. It was difficult to be specific, due to the lack of witnesses and hard evidence. Doubts began creeping into his mind. What was wrong with him today? He was never usually so up and down with his mood. Here he was, deeply rooted in a potentially huge case, and he was doubting himself. He felt like he needed shaking. *Snap out of it, man. Get over yourself. You are not the one wrapped in sheets in some dank basement. You are a detective, investigating a disappearance, murder and long-term fugitive. You. Are. In. Charge.*

He rolled his eyes at himself. His thoughts made him sound like Gary Vaynerchuck, the irritating motivational speaker. Cheesy words were not the answer. He just needed to get on with work. Deal with what he knew and what he wanted to know. The only way to get that right now was to effectively interview the suspect: evil child-killer, Gilbert Winter. A sick, twisted, devious, lying, murdering, bastard. Prison was too good for people like him. Like most police officers he knew, Jain believed that prison was just another word for free hotel. Where the dregs of society who should not be allowed their freedom lived. In some cases, he thought they should bring the death penalty back. People like Winter, child killers and paedophiles should be hung by their balls until they died a painful death. There were some people who just should not be allowed to enjoy the freedoms of prison, he confirmed to himself. No, they got TVs, PlayStations, exercise, fresh air, free food, accommodation, and in most cases it was better than the life they had on the outside—so where was the incentive not to be a criminal?

Jain did not consider that maybe, if their life on the outside was not so miserable, if society contributed more evenly to people, or if the media did not demonise the poor, then prison may not be a more desirable place than their homes in free society. That was liberal hogwash, according to the message he aligned himself with. A message that was increasingly dominating the press and the briefing rooms, which managed to confirm the biases he already held. He did meet some police officers, usually new ones, that came in with an idealistic attitude. They thought that people could be genuinely rehabilitated. They thought that being polite to the criminals and drug addicts made them respect the police more and helped them. They were not so keen, these days, to come into the force on day one and start arresting people. They wanted to talk it over, sit on beanbags and drink tea with suspects. Maybe, they wanted to give them a free house and some cash to get settled with.

Yet again, Jain managed to roll his eyes at himself. Since when had he become Jeremy Kyle? He was far more jaded than he realised.

Saving him from his own thoughts, the stairs creaked and the door swung open. A woman, presumably DS Manos, entered the room. She was around forty years of age, medium-build, medium-height, medium brown hair, medium length and was reasonably—medium—attractive. He did not know what he had expected, but she was very ordinary. That was probably a good thing, he realised, considering how much he had started objectifying every woman he met recently. He really needed to work on that. He was starting to turn into every police officer trope he used to hate.

He smiled at the oncoming DS Medium, and held his hand out ready. She shook it, with a medium-strength grip, and smiled back with a medium-intensity smile.

"Hi, I'm DS Manos. Inspector Baron asked me to come over. He gave me the rundown. Sounds quite shocking."

"Shocking is the right word. The whole situation went from weird to plain insane in the space of a few hours. I'm just putting an interview plan together. Do you want to lead, as you're the senior officer?"

"No. You're the one with the knowledge. I'm not worried about seniority or anything like that. I'll get up to speed and be the secondary."

"OK, fair enough."

Jain thought Manos seemed very down to earth. She had a confidence about her that most female sergeants had. You needed confidence to get ahead in the force as a woman. It was still a man's world and was very slow to change. He explained to her what was said, or not said, in the first interview and what new information he wanted to ask about now. She listened intently, never interrupting. When he finished talking he saw that she had written copious notes in her notebook. She worked with him for the next half an hour, helping him to hash out some other questions for the interview, anticipating 'no comment' for the second time today.

Chapter 29

Mark and his dog remained in situ as the rest of the team did their work. Spotlights had been set up alongside a small, portable generator, and a group of white-suited crime scene investigators surrounded the suspicious mound they had earlier discovered. As they slowly dug away at various points, trying to establish the contents without disturbing them, other officers took photographs and wrote on clipboards. How funny it would be, Mark thought, if they dug up a pet rabbit. All this fuss and seriousness, not to mention the cost. The butterflies in his stomach did not match his self-made comedy. His body chemistry told the truth, and the truth was that this was serious. Very serious indeed. No amount of light-hearted deflection was going to change the fact that something was under that dirt, and according to his panting partner, it was human.

All sorts of images started to race into his mind. He visualised body parts chopped into compact sizes, wrapped in plastic and dumped beside the trees. He imagined a child, limp and lifeless being lifted from a hole in the ground. He pushed the thoughts away and stroked his faithful companion. This was no time to grow a heart.

Eventually, one of the CSI team called out to stop. He, or she—Mark could not tell properly—had found something. A female voice began to speak from under the mask, indicating that it was a 'she' and she could see a foreign object under the dirt. The team worked together to carefully uncover more of the object, moving around each other in silent partnership. As the earth was dusted away, an object came into clear view: a face.

With each movement of the highly-trained officers, more of the face was uncovered. It was a man's face, with dark hair. Mark watched as the rest of the body was slowly revealed, like a twisted scratch card from a Halloween lottery. The body was definitely a man's, and it was definitely quite fresh.

Chapter 30

Jain and Manos were talking like old friends already. They had finished planning the interview and were just waiting for the go ahead message from Inspector Baron. In the meantime, they both swapped stories of their years in the force, keeping the mood light, steering away from tales of death. Manos, it transpired, had transferred in from Gloucester, a neighbouring force, in order to get promoted. She had been a sergeant for two years, working domestic violence and child abuse. Jain felt grateful to have her here now, being more than qualified to deal with something like this. As their stories started to wind down and the conversation grew stilted, the phone rang to save them. It was Inspector Baron, with the update they needed but did not want.

Replying to a question, Jain said, "He was described as white male, about five-foot-ten, short dark brown hair, thirty years of age, no tattoos. She didn't know what he was wearing today."

"Well," responded Baron, "there's a body here that is a male around that age with dark hair. He has a cut on the scalp, small but visible. Given the blood result and the freshness of the body, I want you to go with the assumption it is him until we've had identification and a formal post-mortem. At the end of the day, it's a human body in the ground where Winter works. The body was not alone. There was rope around the neck area and there are signs of bruising all around the neck and burst capillaries in the eyes to indicate strangulation. Again, we need a PM to confirm all this, so just see what he says in interview before revealing anything."

"Yes, boss." Jain felt a bit sick now. It had gone from possible to real too quickly.

"I will arrange a family liaison officer to contact the family of Lockedon. We can't get them to come here to identify the body, but we can't dig him up too quickly until CSI finish their work either. We will get the coroner to take him to the mortuary when possible, and we can get them to identify him then. Terrible business."

With that final comment, Baron signed off the radio. Jain explained to Manos what he had been told and she nodded along, frowning more the longer he continued. Both detectives stood up solemnly, no longer speaking and picked up their paperwork. They remained silent as they walked out of the CID office. The only sound they each heard on their way to the custody suite was the familiar creak of the ageing staircase.

The custody unit was a different matter. No matter what time of day you entered, it was always the same. Windowless, artificially-lit and noisy. Banging on cell doors was accompanied by shouting for drinks or telephone calls. Keyboards were tapped and someone was always in the office, asking for a decision about bail or charging someone.

This familiar scene removed some of the anxiety from Jain's stomach, knowing now that his worst fears of the past twenty-four hours had been confirmed. Not 100%, but close enough for him to bet his meagre savings on. He spoke to the sergeant, who was clearly winding down and getting ready for home time. The night tour sergeant was already here, ready to take over. DS Manos introduced herself to Allard, and she asked for the suspect to be taken to the interview room with his solicitor. No further disclosure was going to be given to her at this time.

Jain and Manos took the usual set of tapes into the interview and started labelling them up in preparation. Less than fifteen minutes later, the faces of Winter and his grumpy solicitor came through the door. They sat down in the same seats as before, and the game began all over again. Jain started the tapes, did his thorough speech of an introduction, introduced his colleague and asked the first question. As expected, Winter gave no comment, and Jain continued to ask simple, factual questions about his whereabouts and who he had contact with, who he lived with and his relationship with the Macallisters, all to the same response: "No comment." Jain looked at Manos and pointed to a section of his interview plan. She nodded. He turned to the two silent opponents and introduced a new question, framed in a revelation.

"Mr Winter. How do you account for the fact that, upon searching Neates House this afternoon, two human bodies were found in the basement? Both bodies were wrapped in bedclothes by someone else, and placed there quite some time ago. Please explain that."

Immediately, the solicitor stepped in.

"Er, that was not disclosed to us, and I would like the time to confer with my client." She looked at Winter, who remained silent. Jain was about to stop the tapes for them to consult, when the tall man finally spoke.

"No. It's ok. We don't need to do that." He looked at the solicitor, and it seemed as though she was about to protest.

Jain looked at Winter with a determined gaze. He had something he needed to say before the old bastard continued.

"Mr Winter, at this stage I must inform you that you are, of course, still under caution. You are also being further arrested on suspicion of the murders of Edward and Lydia Macallister. Your detention has already been authorised for questioning about this. Your rights are the same as before. Do you understand?"

"It's not my fault," Winter continued. "They were very old and suffering every day. They wanted to die."

"Stop talking," the solicitor interrupted.

"Let him talk if he wants to," Manos interjected, "this is his interview after all, not yours, as I believe my colleague made clear to you earlier."

Jain smiled at this. She had laughed when he told her how strict he had been with the solicitor earlier that day. Winter interrupted the moment.

"I'm tired of all this," he murmured. "I'm tired of getting the blame for everything. I always get the blame for everything."

Jain brought everyone's attention back to the key question, and asked Winter very directly, "What did you mean when you said 'they wanted to die'? Did you kill them?"

Winter looked at the two detectives and spoke slowly.

"I will explain. Please don't interrupt. I don't want to have to say it all again. Just listen. Alright?" He looked at them, expecting a response. They nodded.

"I was not lying. I did work for the Macallisters. I was their gardener. I used to be homeless, and lived in a tent in the fields nearby. I eventually got up the courage to talk to them when I saw them in their gardens. They looked like it was too difficult, so I thought I could make some money off them. They agreed. I did my job. Eventually, I did more jobs. Some shopping, some DIY, bits and bobs. They were not getting on well with things. They had a lot of health problems. Anyway, the point is, they wanted to die, but they wanted to die together. They asked me to help them. I said no. I thought they wanted me to bash them to death or something. They had it all planned out. They had this book—you'll find it in the house if you look in their bedroom—called 'The Peacefull Pill'. It showed them what to do. They asked me to help them."

He paused then, taking a sip of water from his plastic cup on the table. Hands trembling slightly. Silence filled the room. No one dared speak whilst he drank, in case it caused him to clam up again. After a few long sips, he continued to talk.

"The book told them that they could go peacefully, together. They just needed some stuff to get it done. They asked me to get it for them. I agreed and they paid for it. I had to go to the party outfits shop in town and buy two of those big cans of helium that you use for party balloons, you know? And they needed some oven bags. The really big plastic ones that you cook massive chickens in. When they were ready, they lay on the bed and I helped them get the bags over their heads, tie them up and put the tube in for the gas. It was all planned out by them. I just did what they wanted."

He reached out for some more sips of water before speaking again. Jain really wanted to interrupt, test the story and ask for more detail, but he stayed silent.

"A few hours later, I went back in and they'd gone. Died. So, I got rid of the equipment. I was supposed to bury them in the back garden, but it was summertime, and the ground was really hard. So, I used the bed stuff to carry them downstairs and into the basement. It wasn't long before they started to smell. Really bad. So, I ended up just leaving them down there. Putting the rug over the entrance and left it. The smell sort of went away after a while. But I didn't move them after that."

This revelation stunned Jain. The man had just confessed to wilfully killing and concealing the husband and wife. He was remorseless. Did he think his cooked-up story about assisted suicide was going to do him any good? The bastard murdered them both and dumped them. His stupid story was not going to help him. Manos summarised what they had been told, trying to keep the incredulity out of her voice, and let Winter confirm that everything he had said was correct. Shaking his head, Jain turned to his partner and asked her if she had any related questions. She shook her head. He looked over at the solicitor, who was furiously scribbling in her legal pad, but made no attempt to speak. Jain slipped a professional voice on and entered interviewer mode again.

"Thank you, Mr Winter, for your candour. There are some more questions. I want to ask you again about Mr Lockedon. The missing person, who I previously asked you about. I am still at a loss as to why you said you had neither seen nor heard of him. We have discovered evidence that you did encounter him recently. Please tell me the truth. Can you elaborate on his disappearance for me?"

Whilst asking this question, Jain knew he was stretching his own truth. He believed what he was saying to be true, but could not exactly prove anything at this stage. The solicitor suddenly stopped writing, and was about to speak. As if she anticipated the response, she quickly closed her mouth and returned to her legal pad.

"So. You found him then?" was all Winter said, looking glumly at the desk.

"What do you mean by that? What do you think we found?" Asked Jain, knowing full well that he had this soulless creature in front of him completely bang-to-rights.

"Jeff. That's what he said his name was. I buried him in the gardens. But, it's not what you think."

He spoke slowly again, quietly now, and looked as though he had completely given up.

"So, you admit burying his body. How did you kill him? Why did you kill him?" Jain asked, amazed at how he could speak of murder so lackadaisically.

"No. No. No. You're not listening to me. I am not taking the blame for things I didn't do anymore. Alright? Just listen and stop talking."

Winter looked tired. He picked up the plastic cup for another sip. It was empty. Manos wordlessly refilled it. He drank and breathed heavily through his nose, preparing his lungs again.

"Jeff, or 'James' apparently, came to the house. It was pouring down with rain. He was snooping around, trying to get in. I wasn't going to speak to him, but I wanted him to go away, so I offered him a cup of tea in the shed. I told him no-one was home and there was no phone signal there. I reckoned he'd walk off down the road. I came back to the shed and he was gone. Job done, I thought. Anyway, I saw, down the gardens at the far end, something in a tree, swinging around. I walked down there. I can't run anymore thanks to prison injuries. And, there he was. He was just hanging there, swinging. He'd taken my ropes and step-ladder from the shed and hanged himself. I couldn't leave him there. I stepped up and cut the rope off the branch. I didn't know what the hell to do with him. I couldn't call the police or you'd find out who I was and about the Macallisters so I just buried him in the softest spot I could find down by them trees."

Jain stared at Winter, open-mouthed and wide-eyed. What an absolute load of bollocks, he thought. Why on earth would a perfectly normal man, with a job, with a girlfriend, with loving parents and a regular life come to some empty house in the middle of nowhere and hang himself? It beggared belief. Manos, too, was looking at Winter, her expression more one of curiosity than disbelief. Manos saw that Jain was lost for words, so she filled the silence.

"Mr Winter. You understand that this is an extraordinary story you're telling us. People all around you seem to become suicidal. I'm not calling you a liar, but I am trying to understand what's happened. You also need to be informed that, on top of the other offences, you are now being further arrested on suspicion of the murder of James Lockedon. You remain under caution, and all your rights are the same. You can exercise them at any time. But, I want to continue with the interview, and I think you do too. Did Mr Lockedon seem depressed to you? Did he do or say anything to indicate he wanted to kill himself?" Manos scribbled furiously as she spoke.

"Well, he hanged himself, so I guess that's a sign." Winter said, apparently not attempting to be humorous.

Jain jumped back in.

"Wait a minute. Don't get clever. Are we expected to believe that three people at that location all just wanted to die and you were innocent? That a random stranger came to your shed and then decided to commit suicide? Is that what you're saying?"

"That is not just what I'm saying. That is what happened. To answer your friend's question, he did seem miserable but most people do these days. He didn't just come to my shed to kill himself. He said his car broke down. Maybe he'd intended to kill himself already and just found the opportunity. Who knows? We'll never know. He'll have to answer to God now. He's the only one who knows the real truth about anything."

Jain and Manos both looked at each other, conferring quietly. They had heard far more than they ever expected and needed to explore Winter's story further. They continued to quiz him about the deaths, and in answer to each question he gave them a long, detailed response. Everything he said, in practical terms at least, matched with what they knew, except for the fact they believed he had carried out the killings himself and with murderous intent.

It was a very unusual interview. The man knew he was going to prison. He was not young and, in all likelihood, would never be free again, so why lie about it in this way? Killing the old couple was still a crime, regardless of how they wanted to go. Concealing Lockedon's body was also a serious crime, even before getting to the cause of death. Winter was going to prison straight from this station, maybe via a court, but certainly without bail. He would never again have a moment of complete freedom. Everyone understood this, yet his story would not budge. He was unmovable on the information he presented. Eventually, they closed down the interview and returned to their office to process what had happened.

Chapter 31

Back in the CID office, Jain and Manos sat on opposite sides of a desk. They were both shuffling paper into neat piles, wondering what to say. The silence was broken by Jain, who clicked on a mouse and brought Google up on a computer screen.

"I want to know about this murder he was in prison for."

He started typing as he rambled on. Manos stopped rifling through paper and looked at him, silently.

"According to PNC, he was done for murder of a child and sexual assault. A pretty sick pair of crimes, with one named victim. But, it doesn't have much detail. Presumably, it was paper-based and converted to digital quite a while later," he continued to type as he talked, making many typos on the screen. Up came a news archive from the Evening Herald.

"Here we go." Both officers looked at the screen. A newspaper article from before either of them were born. They read it in silence.

The Evening Herald.
8 January, 1983

KILLER'S COURT CASE BEGINS TODAY

The arrest of Gilbert Winter last September sent
shockwaves through the local community. The young
adult, unemployed and homeless, was arrested in the
area of Marston Green for sexually assaulting and
murdering local schoolgirl, Natalie Bonner. The
heartless killer was found next to her body, with her
clothes torn and his hands covered in blood. The case
is set for a Jury trial, with the suspect expected to
maintain his innocence.

The article lacked specific details, telling them what they already knew. Jain continued searching for the court papers, specifically looking for any transcripts. Eventually, he found the judge's final summing up following Winter's guilty finding. His comments were pretty damning:

"Natalie died at your hands. Her death was a tragedy for her and for her family, a waste of a promising, young life. Her family's dignity throughout this process has been deeply impressive to any of us who have seen it. The way they have behaved has been a standing reproach to you, Mr Winter, who killed their daughter and abused her body. The impact on them and Natalie's brother, who witnessed your assault, is enormous. The evidence was clear and your lack of willingness to accept responsibility is reprehensible. It has been shown that you tore at her clothes, touched her inappropriately and, when she tried to escape, used a rock to crack her skull. The details are shocking to anyone.

There is only one sentence for murder, in your case detention for life, in formal language detention at Her Majesty's pleasure, and that is the sentence I shall pass upon you.

It is necessary for me to set a minimum period to be served, before you can be eligible for release on licence.

As I think has now become well known, this period is not the period you will serve. It is the minimum period you will serve, before you may even be considered for release. The decision whether you may ever be released will be taken many years from now and will reflect whether you are then thought to represent a risk to the public."

The two detectives now understood what they were dealing with. Sat downstairs, they confidently believed, was a man who could willingly harm an innocent girl, murdering her when he thought she would escape. A man who, when faced with the truth, lied through his teeth.

The depth of depravity sat deep and sickly in their stomachs. A feeling of hatred burned in their chests. Both officers were determined to see this killer get everything that was coming to him, and more. They discussed the paperwork that needed to be completed, sharing the workload evenly. They needed as much as possible to be completed before they could go to the Crown Prosecution Service asking them to charge him with the full offences of murder times three. At this time of night, that would mean telephone calls, emails and faxes to a solicitor, who would then read the reports and make a decision. It all hung on the words they began to write, and the way in which they explained the crime. They made sure that their report was as detailed and sinister as possible.

Chapter 32

Gilbert was alone again. He felt both nervous and relieved at the same time. His guilt over the Macallisters was gone somewhat, now that he had shared their story. He felt bad for them, wanting to die, but knew he had done what they really thought was best to end their long-suffering existence. He did not feel guilty about that, but knew they deserved a proper burial, which they would now get. As for Lockedon, he was still angry about that man. He imposed his suffering upon Gilbert, choosing that location to end his life. It was not my fault, Gilbert thought, that the body had to be hidden. It was Lockedon's, for being so selfish. So what if the man was depressed. Go and do it somewhere else. Now he had ruined other people's lives. Gilbert pondered the past, always dwelling on the actions of others. Humans were so selfish. They were so eager to please themselves at the expense of him. Just because he was different, homeless and an easy target.

He knew, from watching Jain's face in the interview, that the officer had already made up his mind. He already believed what everyone else believed, referring to Gilbert as a sex offender confirmed his bias. Everything from that day had affected each day that followed. His freedom was stolen and his life was sent down a path that was not of his own making. He should have run away from those children. He should have learned to control his anger. If only he could go back to that day and make a different decision. His life would still have been tough, but it would have been so different.

Chapter 33

7 September 1982. Six PM.

Birmingham in the seventies and eighties was a tough place to grow up for most people. The economy was not great, jobs were not plentiful, education was average at best and social tensions were high. Nevertheless, children were afforded the freedom to play and explore, leaving their parents to worry about the pressures of daily life. There were plenty of fields and parks for these kids to play in, after school had finished for the day and their parents relaxed in front of the TV's four solitary channels. There used to be only three, but Channel 4 had recently arrived, increasing their viewing potential by a whole extra third. Those lucky Brits.

The area of Marston Green was typical of Birmingham. Plenty of working class families with average schools, parks and fields for their children to play in. The evenings were getting darker, earlier, with street lights flooding every path by six o'clock. There were no street lights in the woods, however, and kids loved to go where they were not allowed.

Six children were playing together, in a park in Marston Green, making use of the old-fashioned, solid metal swings, roundabout and slides. They were getting a bit old for this equipment, but they always came here anyway. It was either this or down by the garages, which nowadays smelled of urine and looked like a bad artist's spray-painted canvas. All six of these kids were from the same primary school and their parents had known each other since their own childhoods. They were part of a close-knit community; old-fashioned, down-to-earth, living on paycheques week to week, but not as poor as some. The kids rarely changed out of their school uniforms in the evenings, so they were running around and getting sweaty in their grey trousers, white shirts, grey v-neck sweaters and black Clark's shoes. If any people were nearby to hear them, which there were not, then they would have heard the infectious laughter of children, who thought they were more mature than they were. A few choice phrases occasionally slipped past their lips, learned from their parents' private conversations. They were regular children, from regular homes, doing regular things. They were also getting bored.

One of the six, the '*coolest*' boy of the group, who was not really 'cool' in the modern sense but was the one with the confidence, said, "Let's go in the woods. Apparently, there's a dead body in there. It's been there since forever. Truth."

The others were apprehensive, not believing the story but still scared enough of dark places. But, of course, no-one wanted to admit they were scared, so off they went. Walking across the park, onto the grass and through the unkempt field, they saw the line of trees as a natural barrier between them and the noisy, grey world of cars. It had always held a mystery, simply because they had been told not to go in there. There were two reasons for this: the parent's reason that it was full of smackheads and needles and the children's reason that it was haunted or populated by dead bodies. Neither reason was strictly true, although drug users would sometimes go there to avoid the police.

On this day, there was only one occupant of the woods. A young, thin, tall man living in a tent. Gilbert Winter had taken up a space between the trees, camping there in his grubby old tent, as he had often done in similar places all around the Midlands. He was neither a smackhead nor a ghost, but he looked a bit like both, thanks to malnutrition and a naturally gaunt appearance. As always, he wanted two things: to be left alone and to listen to his radio. Until six pm he had been able to do both.

The children walked past the initial tree line and went further in to the darkening enclosure. All were scared, but none would admit it. They were not babies. Another year and they would be finishing primary school. They were big kids in their own eyes. They walked closely together, kicking at tree stumps, snapping stray branches and looking behind themselves at every opportunity. The cool kid stopped and the others followed suit. He whispered, "Look. Over there. I told you there was a dead body." He was pointing at a shape not far away, but in darkness and cover it was had to see fully. It was Gilbert in his tent. More specifically, it was Gilbert's feet sticking out of the tent. He had fallen asleep listening to his radio. He was lying on his back inside the tent, with his legs protruding through the unzipped entrance. A mound of dry sticks were propped near them, as a makeshift bonfire, which had not yet been lit.

The group of children, lead by 'cool kid', approached the site quietly. Natalie Bonner followed along, wondering what they were supposed to be doing. She really did not want to see a dead body. As they got closer, they all heard the sound of the quiet radio. It's fuzzy reception playing the tunes of that week's pop charts. 'Eye of the Tiger' by Survivor was apparently a big hit that week. Natalie was not a fan, although she had often heard her parents singing along to it, which only served to make it less cool.

Slowly, carefully, Cool Kid lead the group to the body. They were right next to the tent when Natalie heard her name.

"Nat. Check if it's really dead." Cool kid whispered. She looked at him in disgust.

"No way. I'm not touching it. You do it."

"Go on. I'll give a tenner."

"You haven't got a tenner."

"I have. I promise. I've got loads of money at home. I'll give you a tenner if you touch it. Don't be a wuss."

Her heart was pounding. Being dared to do something was hard to turn down if you wanted to save face. The ridicule of being a 'wuss' was pretty bad. She tried to turn it around.

"You do it then unless you're a wuss."

"You're a wuss," came cool kid's ever-so-clever response.

Natalie felt trapped. She really did not want to touch it. She would take any other dare but there were none to take. The alternative, playground mockery, was not a choice worth taking either. Sighing, she stepped forward and touched a shoe.

A voice from the back of the group, a spot of relative safety, chimed in.

"That's not touching the body. You've got to touch the body. Touch his face or something."

Natalie was still bent over and looked back at the group. They were all staring at the man intently. Believing that she had little choice, she crouched down onto her knees and reached further inside. Her fingers prodded at the dead man's stomach. She looked back, having done the dare. She withdrew her hand and knelt upright, triumphant. Suddenly, the corpse's hand grabbed her arm. Natalie froze with her mouth wide open. No noise came out. The other children shouted, Cool Kid included, swearing with words they would get smacked for using. They all started running as fast as their legs could carry them; running back to the safety of the playground and its solid metal death traps.

All except Natalie, whose frozen body was in the grip of the dead man's hand. She started to pull away but he did not let go. Gilbert had been awoken by unknowns. In his mind they were drug addicts coming to steal his meagre possessions. He would not let anyone do that again. He held on tight to the girl, not registering her age or gender at first. Natalie shouted at him to let her go and he realised what she was: a child.

Confused, he loosened his grip and she flew backwards, landing head first in his homemade bonfire. It was unlit, but her head still bashed hard against the wood and rocks surrounding it. Gilbert stood upright, quickly exiting his home. Natalie was pulling herself up to her knees. There was blood above her eye and she was moving slowly. The blood was trickling down onto her mouth, pooling between her closed lips. He walked to her and tried to touch the blood, drawn to it, as he always had been. As his finger touched her mouth, she bit him and turned to run. She could not see properly and tripped again, landing on her knees and tearing her cheap grey trousers. Gilbert's anger flooded his system. His uncontrolled rage bubbled up to the surface, as it always did when he felt humiliated. He grabbed the girl by her shirt collar and pulled. She stood upright and tried to kick him, missing by inches. Twisting and pulling, her v-neck sweater, which had been tied around her waist, fell to the ground in a limp polyester puddle. The top button of her shirt popped off in protest at being pulled in too many directions. Gilbert used his free hand to reach for her shoulder and panic flooded her system. The adrenaline gave her enough strength to break free, free of his grip and—thanks to the fragile plastic buttons—free of her school shirt.

Gilbert's arm remained extended, holding nothing but a small, white blouse. Natalie was free of his grip, but she was not in possession of her balance. She fell again, landing on her back, with the back of her head hitting the ground first.

The ground was not forgiving and the rocks embedded in it even less so. Her skull landed fully on the solid grey rock with a sickening crack. The rock only jutted out from the soil an inch, but that was more than enough to render her unconscious as soon as she landed. She began to twitch and vomit. Chunks of bile-soaked food came up her oesophagus and tried to exit her body.

Gravity refused to help and everything remained in her mouth and throat. She unconsciously tried to swallow, but was only partially successful. With her airway fully blocked she began to choke.

Gilbert stood and watched, gripped in his own state of panic. He had no idea what was going on. All he knew was that some shapes ran away and this girl had been in his tent. She was clearly injured and something bad was happening, but he had no knowledge of what or how to fix it. He knelt down next to her and saw that her mouth was full of a vile-smelling soup. He tried to turn her head, which did nothing to help. He shook her shoulders and slapped her face trying to wake her up. Nothing changed. She continued to make animal noises and strange movements for a minute or two, then stopped.

Gilbert was still on his knees looking at the girl. His eyes had adjusted to the low light and he could see her fully now. She was very young. He guessed at about nine or ten years old. Her face was partially blood stained, as were sections of her hair. Blood, spit, vomit and unknown liquids were encased in her mouth, ears and neck creases. She was completely topless. She had a small flat stomach, pale skin, undeveloped mounds of breast and skinny arms. Her body was dirty from where she had fallen and where his hands had touched to shake her awake. She was clearly dead.

He was still in a world halfway between groggy sleep and adrenaline excitement. He had no concept of time, not knowing what the time was or how long had passed since the girl's friends had run away. It would not be long before someone returned for her. There was nowhere safe to go. No way for him to call the police or an ambulance, not that he really wanted to do either. He hated the police and there was nothing much an ambulance could do now. Feeling around her neck for a pulse, his suspicions were confirmed. Her body was completely devoid of movement, internal or external. Her last breath had been expelled before the passageways to her lungs had been blocked by the contents of her stomach. She looked so young now. So innocent, despite what had happened. Gilbert never cried, but he felt like it now. He knew that this was bad. His life in general had been bad, but this was definitely not going to end well for him. He picked up the body, not wanting to leave it so exposed, and carried the girl back to his tent. There he sat, waiting, silent tears falling. The girl lay on the floor in front of him, also waiting silently, but unable to cry anymore.

Chapter 34
Tuesday, 22 May, 11PM

Mr and Mrs Lockedon sat quietly as the family liaison officer explained the situation. It was possible, the officer said, that their son had been found. Their minds raced with images of his his lifeless body. They both rejected such thoughts in absolute, defiant disbelief. There was no way that this had happened to their son. The police were mistaken and some other unfortunate soul was currently occupying a shallow grave after being murdered. It was a terrible circumstance, but not their concern. James was still out there somewhere, and it was the police's job to find him. All of these thoughts filled their heads, but their mouths remained closed. The officer finished explaining things and talked about mortuaries, identification and post-mortems.

Mairi Lockedon tried to deny what she heard and looked at her husband. She could see the tension in his jaw as he struggled to hide his emotions. His eyes were glassy and he was constantly swallowing. *He believes them*, Mairi thought. She looked over at Claire, who was now staying with them until James returned. *She won't be taken in by this*, Mairi was sure. But, as she looked at Claire and caught her eye, the young girl collapsed into floods of tears and guttural sobs. *What's going on?* Mairi thought. Denial was a powerful force of the mind, but the truth was now difficult to ignore. The police were sure, her husband seemed sure and even the strong and supportive Claire believed it. Maybe it really was James. In some ways it made sense. *Where else would he be? He would never have cut everyone off without a word, would he?* No. Not James.

In that moment, denial released its lock on the gate to Mairi's logic and she joined the others in heartbreaking knowledge and tragic misery.

Chapter 35

Jain had received the email from the CPS. A
confirmed trio of charges, subject to finalisation of the
paperwork and file submission. He and Manos triumphantly
returned to the custody unit to share the good news. In the
office was the night tour sergeant. Allard had since gone
home. Tonight's lucky winner of the 'charge an evil
murderer prize' was newly-promoted sergeant Westwood.
Westwood was a female sergeant in her first six-months of
custody duties. She seemed to hate everything about it: the
lack of natural light, the complaining prisoners, the
complaining officers, the bureaucracy. She would do
anything to get into another unit as a sergeant.
Unfortunately, with promotion came compromise, and if she
wanted three stripes on her shoulder then she had to take
the post.

Thankfully, Baron had not gone home and was doing
overtime to see the job through. He was sat in the custody
unity with the sergeant and detention officer, waiting for
Jain and Manos to return with the CPS report.

"All charges agreed. I've written up the MG3. We're
good to go."

Baron smiled, grateful that the CPS could see the
situation and were not asking for the world before giving a
decision, as they sometimes did.

"Nice one. Pretty much bang to rights apart from his
bullshit story about suicides. I've spoken to the bosses and
he will have to go to court first thing, but that's just a
formality. He will then be taken to HMP Grendon to serve

out the rest of his miserable life. This is the icing on the cake. They'll arrange a court case, obviously, but unless he's a complete idiot there would be no reason to plead 'not guilty'. It's not as if he's ever getting out again."

Manos spoke up as the last sentence began to sink in.

"Did you read up on his original case? Why on earth did they even let him out to begin with?"

"Yeah, I was in the job when it happened, heard all about it. Apparently, he snatched a girl from a group of friends one evening after school. Took her to his tent and tried to touch her up. She tried to escape so he bashed her head in. All of her friends gave evidence to confirm he'd snatched her and ran off with her into the woods. Total freak. That's the problem with society though. They always think people can be rehabilitated and deserve a second chance. Well, this fucker isn't getting another chance, not after this. They ought to bring back hanging."

Manos and Jain agreed. In their view, Winter deserved to hang, especially after what he had done to James Lockedon. His girlfriend and parents were apparently destroyed at the news. Winter should be made to see their faces and take in the tragedy he had caused. There was such evil in the world. Jain added to what the Inspector had said.

"Thanks to modern technology. If it wasn't for that blood analysis, they might never have got justice. He's getting what he deserves, but it's nice to know we managed to pin everything on him that he's guilty of. I hope there are no more bodies out there thanks to this nutter."

Baron nodded in agreement, "It doesn't bear thinking about. Let's bring him to the desk please, sergeant."

As Winter arrived at the sergeant's desk, all of the officers present in the unit stood around and watched, judging. He stood silent, bare-footed in front of the computer screen.

"Listen to the officer, please," said Westwood, then nodded at Jain.

"Gilbert Andrew Winter, you are being charged that at Neates House, A369, Somerset, at an unknown time and date, you did, of sound mind and discretion, unlawfully kill both Ian and Gail Macallister with the intent to kill or cause grievous bodily harm. You are also charged that on the 20th of May 2019, at Neates House, A369, Somerset, at an unknown time you did, of sound mind and discretion, unlawfully kill James Lockedon, with the intent to kill or cause grievous bodily harm, contrary to common law."

As Jain read through the wordy charge sheet and finally cautioned Winter, the tall man remained passive and distant. He listened without hearing and thought of being back in his cell. Yet again, he was being labelled, blamed and punished for crimes he had not committed. He was not innocent of every crime on his record, he knew that, but had never intentionally 'murdered' someone.

The Macallisters were different, he was really helping them and believed it a hundred percent. It was futile to argue with the police—the authorities. Winter was, under any circumstances, going back to prison, so what's the point in arguing any more?.

All he knew and cared about at that moment, was that he was not going back to Merryweather Prison. Never again would he look at that place, or the people in it.

Chapter 36

Night turned back into day, new officers arrived at the station and Jain could finally go home. Everything had been handed over to the day tour CID. The file prep, paperwork and long list of bureaucratic tasks were in their hands now. Gilbert Winter was awaiting his private police taxi to a life of incarceration and the detective could enjoy some days off.

Manos returned to her sector, having played her role in the investigation of a dangerous killer and CSI kept on at the scene, sweeping for any additional evidence.

Further days turned into long, busy nights on repeat and everything went back to normal. Normal for everyone except Winter, who after a long spell of freedom and relative safety at the Macallister's estate, was back in prison. He felt isolated and depressed. Things were different at Grendon than Merryweather. CCTV cameras were everywhere. The guards were a bit more polite and no-one was trying to kill him. He kept himself to himself as always, hoping that none of the other inmates asked too much about him. The downside to all the CCTV was that the guards rarely seemed to be paying attention to anyone and stood around the walls a lot, staring into space.

As time went on, a new solicitor came to visit Winter. They discussed court proceedings and strategy, but Winter had no more time for that. He explained that there was no point in fighting it. He had no fight left. He just wanted to be left alone. Signed paperwork was submitted and he attended a short court hearing to plead guilty before a judge. Doing so made him feel ashamed. Not because of the charges against him, but because he knew it was not true. He could see the way people looked at him, judging him from their padded seats: *killer, child killer, pensioner killer, home stealer, psycho,* he assumed they thought. There was very little press coverage, which was a surprise to him, but a pleasant one.

Following the end of court and return to prison, Winter went back to his cell to read. He enjoyed books, especially ones about gardening, he discovered. He was lucky to have a cell and bunk bed all to himself, albeit temporarily. He was lucky. The irony of that thought was not lost on him and he smiled a crooked grin. He set about tidying up his belongings, placing them on the small shelf and started folding back his bedsheets. Sleep was all he ever really wanted to do these days. Something inside him had been broken after Detective Jain had arrested him. Any more desire to live a free life or keep moving around, living in tents was gone. This would be his last home and that was just fine.

The bedsheets in Grendon were much nicer than Merryweather. They were cleaner, thinner, more comfortable and crisp. He folded them back again and sat on the mattress arranging himself for maximum comfort and privacy. As he twisted the sheets once more and wrapped them against his skin, he thought back to how James Lockedon had looked when he found him. The young man had urinated himself, that much was obvious. Gilbert would hopefully not suffer that embarrassment. He had emptied his insides as much as possible just a few minutes earlier.

The sheet was tightly wound and securely gripped, leaving Winter to take the final step himself. There were no ceiling fixtures to hang from, so he had to rely on the top bunk's frame taking his own bodyweight as his feet slid along the floor. He knew that he had to cut off the blood supply to the brain or the agony would be long-lasting and unbearable. He wanted to die, but he did not want to suffer.

Everything was prepared as best as he could. He had no cell mate, no passing visitors and a little hope that no one would be in a rush to save him.

Chapter 37

Claire had received a call from Jim's parents that morning. They had received a visit from the family liaison officer again, but this time they had brought Jim's possessions with them. As she arrived at their home, she felt a sense of dread. Looking at Jim's things was not on her most wanted list at the moment. It was enough of a struggle just to get through the day with nothing of his to look at. Despite this, she knew that his parents would want her to come. They were also still grieving hard. Their son had been murdered and they would never have the chance to say goodbye. Their last vision of him had been tainted, seen through a glass window on a metal tray, bloated, twisted, bruised and damaged. All their photos of him were ruined now, as that was the image they would now see.

In the living room sat Mairi, holding a box of clear plastic bags.

"We're going to destroy his clothes," she explained. "They're filthy, but we wanted you to have this. I don't really know how they work and there are probably some photos of you two on there. It won't turn on for me."

Jim's phone was wrapped in plastic, and Claire knew it just needed to be charged up.

"Thanks," she replied, putting it in her handbag. "I'll charge it up at home. If there's any nice pictures on there I'll let you know. Shall I make some tea?'

For the next few hours, they all sat in the Lockedon's lounge drinking tea. They mostly cried together, but sometimes laughed. It was a heartbreaking day, but therapeutic all the same. Claire felt drained of emotion when she left the house. She drove home slowly, remembering that first drive along the A369 to find Jim's car. She hated herself now for feeling angry at the time. She had been so selfish to assume he had cheated on her or abandoned her. The realisation now that he had been murdered by that sicko in Neate's House was the biggest trigger for her. That knowledge made her so angry at herself and at the world. It was so unfair. He had so much to live for and it was all taken away from him. *From us,* she really meant.

When Claire arrived at home, she dropped her keys on the side and went straight to bed. She plugged her phone in to charge and realised she needed another cable for Jim's. Double plugs were set up and both phones lay on her bedside table. In the darkness, she drifted off to sleep.

Within minutes, she was woken up by the sound of vibrating wood. Then she heard her phone ping. Then more pings and more vibrations. Both phones were going wild. She sat up and looked at them. Jim's phone lit up and green bubbles populated the screen. Most of them had her name on, although there were others. She realised that these were the messages she had been sending on the day, which had obviously never gone through due to the lack of signal. She was surprised his phone still had service, before realising it had automatically connected to her WiFi. There were texts, WhatsApp messages, voice messages and missed calls all over his screen. She felt sad for Jim again. He never knew how much people cared and were worried about him.

Claire's own phone was a similar sight. No missed calls, but a trio of WhatsApp messages were in green clouds on her phone's bright screen. She picked up the device and swiped the screen to unlock it. Three WhatsApp messages, all from Jim. The now-charged device had connected to WiFi and started its updates and synchronisation. The messages must have been waiting to send since the day he went missing. She opened the first one.

'I've broken down. Engine might be flooded or something. Do you know anyone that can tow me to a garage?'

Followed by another, once Jim had realised there was no signal.

'I know you're probably trying to get hold of me. I'm not ignoring you. There's no signal here, so this'll get to you when I come into an area with service. Don't go mad! I took the day off sick. Couldn't face that place today. Just need some time to myself. I'll see you soon.'

The third message was much longer and must have taken ages to type. It was like a proper essay at first glance and Claire smiled. He never wrote long messages. He must have been bored, sat in his car, waiting for the rain to stop. She read through it.

'Claire. I wanted to talk about something but never really found the right time. You know that I'm not like other people and

struggle with social situations and my mood. What I never told you is that I've been dealing with this most of my adult life and never wanted to talk about it. Basically, a few years back I went to the doctor and he diagnosed me with clinical depression. He put me on meds and I thought I was getting better. I never really did and I've seen all sorts of doctors and mental health workers, and they've changed my meds a few times. It's a bit embarrassing so I wanted to keep it secret until I found a way to admit it to you. It's a bit pathetic. I used to think about killing myself all the time. Sometimes even when I was at work, I'd go and sit in the loos and try and think of a way to do it that didn't hurt anyone else. I've thought about all sorts of ways. Lately, I've been reading up on it again and planned my way out but kept feeling too guilty about it. I don't want to hurt anyone, but I'm always in so much pain. It's not the kind of pain that you can put a plaster on. It's just always there on the inside. Like fear, nervousness, anxiety, self-hatred, desperation to die and so on, all in one go. It's unbearable sometimes and it's unbearable now. I can't carry on like this anymore. You really deserve someone better and someone who wants a family and can give you a good life. I think today is a bit of a sign. I've found a way to get it done where no-one will get hurt. I know it's selfish. If it's possible, I hate myself even more for causing others to feel some of my pain. But, if anyone knew what it felt like to be like this most of the time then they would understand. Please try to understand. I understand if you can't. Maybe, one day, my parents will understand that the way I am is not their fault, but is mostly down to biology. I don't want anyone to feel as though they made me this way. I can't avoid it any longer. I have to go now. I love you.'

Before finishing the message, Claire's stomach started to turn. She felt faint and although she made it to the end of the text, she immediately rushed to the bathroom. Vomiting into the bowl, it felt as though someone was ripping out her insides. She slumped onto the floor, leaning against the toilet. She felt gutted. Not just metaphorically, but literally gutted. Her insides felt like jelly. Her legs were beneath her, totally numb. It was too much to process. If she tried to stand up, she was sure she would faint.

Jim had taken his own life. She repeated that fact to herself in her head, over and over. She reworded it to try and make more sense. He killed himself. He committed suicide. He hung himself. He died by his own hand. He... None of these interpretations made any more sense than the other. *There must be more to it*, Claire demanded to believe. *He was fine; he had no reason to kill himself.* Her thoughts on this were fixed and no amount of repetition was going to change her mind.

At that moment, she really hated Jim.

Chapter 38

After the court had finished with the finer details of Winter's short-lived case, they began releasing everything from evidence back to the officers in charge. One officer in CID had inherited the task of dealing with the evidence lists, exhibit referencing and all the jobs no-one really wanted when it came to property and evidence. That officer, a keen, young Constable named DC Jenkins, received an email to inform him that everything could now be released.

By 'released', it usually meant 'destroyed'. Very rarely did anyone want to keep something that had been seized by the police and retained as evidence. It was usually dirty, blood-stained, musty or simply unwanted. All DC Jenkins had to do was locate the record and choose for it to be disposed. By the magic of police staff at headquarters, its existence would get erased. Job done. Occasionally, however, exhibits seemed to jump out at him as important or valuable. Technology was an obvious factor, such as computers or mobile phones. These were easily returned to their owners.

Jenkins scrolled through the list from the Winter case for anything that was not to be destroyed. The list was relatively small for a murder enquiry, mostly CSI exhibits, household bedding, tools and one book. That last item jumped out as unusual to Jenkins. One book, by itself, seemed important. Maybe a notebook full of admissions of guilt or a collection of photographs. Intrigued, he clicked on the item and read its full description: *3188TT12 Paperback book. Title: The Peaceful Pill Handbook by Philip Nitschke and Fiona Stewart.* It had been seized by an officer in the police support unit, who had seized a dozen other items. He decided to give him a call.

Upon speaking to the officer—a man with a deep, gruff voice—it became apparent that he had done nothing more than follow orders passed down from above. He did not even remember seizing the book. From checking his pocket notebook it transpired that he had found the book in a bedside table in the master bedroom. It was the only book in the room. He could not, in fact, remember seeing any other books. His supervisor at the time, Sergeant Fraser, had requested he bag and tag the book as he thought the content was suspicious. He had nothing more to add than that, so Jenkins thanked the gruff man and ended the call.

Looking at the record further, Jenkins saw that the book had never been taken out of evidence. No-one had removed it from its bag or requested it be removed from the detained property store for an interview. It had remained in situ, gathering dust, since the day of Winter' arrest. He remembered the name PS Fraser and decided to ask him if it was required for any reason. He called the sergeant directly on his force radio.

"PS Fraser, go ahead."

"Hello sir, it's DC Jenkins from CID. I'm exhibits officer for the Gilbert Winter case. Does that ring a bell with you?"

"Yep. I remember that one. Weird old house. Apparently the gardener murdered the occupants. We seized quite a lot of random stuff."

"That's right. The case has finished and I'm sorting out the evidence we need to get rid of or keep. I spoke to an officer who seized a book and he says you told him to bag it."

"If that's what he says, then it's probably right. What's the issue?"

"No issue. I just need to know what it represents. Is it evidence we need to keep or can it be returned to someone or destroyed et cetera?"

"What's the book called? I can't remember off the top of my head seizing a book."

"Your colleague seized it. The peacefull pill, it's called."

"Oh yeah. That's right. It was in the bedroom. A book that was all about suicide and how to kill yourself. Really weird. I knew they had the gardener in custody and thought he might have been planning to kill himself, so got the book seized for the officers."

"OK. Thanks. Did they ask for it specifically?"

"No. It just seemed relevant. It wasn't like it was in a library full of books. It was next to the bed by itself, obviously being read, so it was relevant in my opinion. I always seize more than we need if there's any doubt. Better to be safe than sorry."

The sergeant sounded like an officer from the army. His tone was stiff and proper, dripping in authority. Jenkins felt quite intimidated.

"OK sir, thanks for that. I assume you no longer require it for any reason then?"

"I never did. I just took it in case it was relevant. Ask the OIC if he ever had any use for it. If not, just bin it."

"Yes, sir. I'll check with him. Thank you."

The call was ended abruptly from the other end. Jenkins was about to click on the dispose button, when he thought to himself that he had already checked with two people, so he may as well check with the last one. The OIC: officer in charge, which turned out to be a Superintendent, given that the case was so serious. However, in reality, it was usually either the arresting officer or the interviewing officer. As thorough as ever, Jenkins ran through the records and found the officer whose name was most regularly typed over the investigation: DC Sajid Jain.

He gave the detective a call. The conversation turned out to be very short and, in the end, he did not click 'dispose'.

Chapter 39

Detective Constable Sajid Jain had performed his usual, sad, bachelor's routine at home. He was fully caffeinated yet barely awake. Arriving at the station, parking the car in a nearby road and groggily walking up the stairs, he was met by the sound of a phone beginning to ring. The urge to let it go was strong, but they were bound to ring back, so he answered the call.

"DC Jain, CID, how can I help?"

"Ah, hello. It's DC Jenkins. We met briefly but you probably don't remember. Anyway, I'm going through the evidence list for Gilbert Winter and disposing of what's no longer required. There's some stuff with your name on, and others you might be able to decide about."

Winter, thought Jain. *That guy will forever haunt my nightmares.* The old gardener had appeared in many of Jain's dreams since the day he was charged. The old man's melancholy demeanour was unsettling. The fact he so obviously thought that nothing was his fault, yet he had murdered numerous people in cold blood. Evil bastard. Jain slept at night with his mind filled with over-the-top images of Winter cutting up bodies of children after he had apparently molested them. The man was evil—it was all in black and white—and his history spoke for itself.

"What's the evidence you need a decision on?" He said, with a dry throat.

"A book. Someone in PSU seized it, but you're the one who was leading the investigation at the time. It's called the peaceful pill. Do you want it kept or disposed of?"

Jain was confused. He had never heard of the book, and certainly had not asked for it to be seized. It was not used in the interviews or referred to in the court files.

"Sorry mate. I don't know anything about that. Why would they seize a book?"

"The supervisor, sergeant Fraser, said it was suspicious. It was in the bedroom and it was all about suicide. He thought maybe Winter was planning to kill himself."

Before speaking, Jain's heart started to pound a tangible rhythm in his chest.

"Suicide?"

"Apparently."

"Don't get rid of it. I'm coming straight over."

Despite not knowing about the book, he remembered exactly what Winter had said in interview. He had told the officers about a book given to him by the Macallisters, who wanted to end their life. He remembered being told about the book detailing their intended suicide and Winter's role in it. He remembered that he had totally ignored the man's story, assuming it was another lie. He had not even looked for the existence of a book. He had, potentially, failed to do his job properly. He rushed out of the office, back down the unstable staircase and into his car.

Whilst driving, his thoughts turned back to Winter's interview. He remembered the details of his suicide pact with the Macallisters. According to the evil gardener, he had been instructed to suffocate them in a 'humane' way with helium and oven bags. Supposedly, that would allow them to die whilst sleeping, painlessly. If this peaceful pill book existed, which it obviously did, and it contained instructions to match Winter's story, then there was a small chance that the murderer had been telling the truth. After all, why else would he know the contents of such a book, and why would he leave it behind?

A sick feeling began to flood his upper body and sweat beaded on his forehead. He was panicking. Maybe, just maybe, he had not killed the old couple in cold blood. Maybe, in an alternate universe, he was really doing them a final favour and had ended their suffering. It was still a crime in this country, though, he remembered. That was little comfort when everything he had known to be true — and based his actions upon — could turn out to be false. The one thing he had promised not to do was let people down. He was supposed to be thorough; investigate every angle. He remembered the woman in the bin. Her investigators had not followed through on their legal obligations and she had ended up dead. Thankfully, Gilbert was already guilty of enough and probably deserved to be in prison.

Probably was not really strong enough, though.

At last, Jain arrived at his destination. A satellite station hosting offices and store rooms. A police station, but only a small one, predominantly for admin purposes. There was no custody unit or response team working out of it. He swiped his access card and let himself in. This was a nice place, he realised. Much cleaner than his own station. It had that smell of a newly built corporate office, with clean carpets and bright lighting. He found his way through to where Jenkins was working and sat down.

"Right. Thanks for calling. Where's this book?"

"Still in the store room. I haven't physically removed it. I'm just doing the digital work at the moment. Wait two minutes and I'll bring it out."

He walked off down the corridor, leaving his PC screen unlocked. Jain looked at the record on the screen: *3188TT12 Paperback book, title: The Peaceful Pill Handbook by Philip Nitschke and Fiona Stewart.* His heart hammered. He hated feeling like this. Why, if Winter was a murderer, did he feel so guilty? The man had convictions and a history of violence. Who cared if two of the murders were not really him? He still technically killed them and what court was going to be lenient when he was already a monster?

Jenkins returned with the book. It was a paperback in a clear plastic bag, sealed closed with a blue clip. Jain ripped it open.

"Hang on a sec," Jenkins reacted, "I need to write down the time you opened it and your force ID number."

He began typing on the keyboard. Jain, undeterred, began to flick through the book's pages. It was a thin book with a cover depicting a beach and a sunset. An oddly innocent visage for such a macabre topic. There were pictures and diagrams, all covering various methods of painless suicide. One chapter described, in great detail, how the inhalation of an oxygen-free gas such as helium would render a subject unconscious and twenty minutes later, lead to death. All that was required were a few deep breaths, whilst the head was sealed in a plastic bag, and the end would come. The complication came with the use of equipment: pipes, bags, canisters and their subsequent disposal, if one cared about the scene they would be found in. That must have been where Gilbert came in.

He thought quickly, furiously and in silence. Jenkins asked if he was alright, to which he gave a curt grunt and a nod of his head. What decision was he going to make? As far as he could tell, he had two realistic options: one, ignore it, leave Winter to rot in jail and let him be punished for the crimes he was guilty of; or two, bring it up as a clear point of evidence in favour of the suspect, leading to a potential mistrial and further investigations. He could even be found innocent. No, no, no, that would certainly not be happening. There was only decision: ignore it.

He turned to Jenkins and said, "Sorry for wasting your time. I thought it was something else. Carry on. Dispose of it. We don't need it." Then left the office, walked out of the station and got back into his car. There, he sat in silence for quite some time, pondering the implications of his actions, past and present.

Chapter 40

Gilbert Winter was pronounced dead at four-thirty in the afternoon. His death was ruled as a suicide. He was the thirtieth male prisoner to commit suicide so far in the year. Last year, the number of suicides by men in prison was eighty three. Gilbert was just another number. It took prison staff nearly two hours to notice that he was hanging in his cell. Not that Gilbert wanted to be saved, but the staff knew they were going to get in trouble. Ultimately, they were sure that their actions would be written off as a result of staff shortages, pressure of the environment and 'further training' would be recommended. No-one would be punished for failing to save the life of a convicted child abuser and multiple murderer. As far as they were concerned he had never contributed to society; he had only taken from it. And, now he was going to take more by having tax payers fund his funeral.

His body was removed and a post-mortem conducted. There was no foul play, according to the coroner, who had filled out most of the paperwork before performing any of his incisions. Winter's body was cremated and no-one came to say goodbye. The ultimate irony of destruction by fire, when it was his only true fear.

Claire was informed of Winter's suicide and went to her bedroom to cry. She was not crying for him. She still felt he was a twisted individual for murdering that old couple in their homes. She was crying because it was yet another reminder of what had happened to Jim; the sadness filled her deeply and completely. She hated Jim for what he had done and she loved him for who he had been. She hated herself for not knowing the pain he had suffered, silently and alone. A pain so severe that the only solution was to die. If only he had shared with her, then surely she could have helped him. She still did not understand the mechanics of his condition and she never would. Gilbert Winter's death only reminded her of what should have happened that day. Jim should have gone to work. She should have gone to see him. They should have gone to bed together and hugged each other to sleep as they always did. If only he had not skipped work. If only. Would anything have been different in the end, though? Her thoughts lead her down a dark path and all she could see was Jim, alone and in pain, too ashamed to tell anyone the truth. His expression of sadness twisted into that of the creepy old gardener. She had never met Winter in person but had seen his face in the papers. He looked like a murdering paedophile, she decided, because that was what he was. And, now, his face was merging with Jim's. Both of them forever linked in her mind by that day and their deaths. If only she could go back in time and say something, do something, be something different. If only.

She brought up Jim's last message on her phone. No-one, she decided, was ever going to know the truth. Her mind was made up. Her decision was final. She ran her finger over the glass screen and pressed 'delete'.

Chapter 41

When Jain returned home from work, he still had Winter on his mind. He had decided to erase any potential for justice from the world. No-one except him now knew the truth about Winter and no-one else ever would. His mind was made up. His decision was final. Knowing that Winter had been Jim's killer was his only consolation. The gardener's ridiculous story that a young man like that would kill himself, especially in such a way in that location, was inconceivable. Winter might have suffered a little injustice, but he had received the right sentence for his other crimes. No-one needed to know the whole truth now. It was in no-one's best interests.

His mobile phone buzzed in his pocket, so he slid it out with his left hand. Holding it in front of him, a number he did not recognise lit up the screen.

"Hello."

"Sajid?"

"Yes."

"Hi. It's Inspector Allard. I just wanted to let you know about Winter. The fucker only went and killed himself yesterday."

Jain's stomach felt as though it had been punched. Sickness swelled up inside him for the second time that day.

"Jesus Christ."

"If we're lucky, he'll be meeting the man downstairs, not upstairs!"

Allard's joke elicited no response from Jain, who simply sat on the sofa with his head bowed.

"So, what does that mean for us?"

"Nothing. The case was finished. It just means he won't be serving his time. He's basically freed himself from prison again. He should be rotting in there, not taking the easy way out. There'll be an investigation, but no-one's gonna be crying any tears for that old boy."

"No. I suppose they won't," Jain replied, knowing that Allard was right. Gilbert Winter's legacy was set in stone. Chiselled in the granite of history as a multiple-murdering homeless sex offender. The worst kind of nightmare for parents across the country. The subject of many a tabloid's headlines. The fuel upon which the fear of crime could feed. He looked like criminal. He was a criminal. He died a criminal. There was no need to feel guilty about that. Jain was not sure he believed his own assertions but there seemed little point in sharing them now.

"OK," Jain continued, thanks for letting me know. Have you told the victim's family?"

"Yeah, already done. I bet they'll be happy with the result. Eye for an eye and all that. Anyway, take it easy. Speak to you later."

Jain let his phone drop onto his coffee table with a clang. He knew that something was wrong here. He cared little for Winter but did have morals. That inner conscience started to scratch away on his insides, poking and prodding with its nauseating finger. Anxiety always started in his stomach until it built up to a constant feeling of dread.

Anxiety about something he had no control over. Winter was dead. Lockedon was dead. The Macallisters were dead. There were no actions he could take to undo any of those realities. Even if he mentioned the suspicion—and that was all he had—that Winter had been telling the truth, it would do nobody any good. Not the deceased, not the police and not the family. Processing his thoughts in that way, no matter how forced his logic felt, caused him to decide on a single course of action: say nothing. He hoped that this decision did not have consequences.

Epilogue
Saturday, 7 September 2019. 10:00AM

The parents of Natalie Bonner sat on opposite sides of a small wooden table in a quaint old coffee shop. They were reading the newspaper together, something they had not done for many years. Silently poring over every word in the article about Gilbert Winter, his recent crimes and subsequent death, they felt their mental scars begin to ache. They knew his name well, never forgetting what he had done to their daughter.

They knew, as did the parents of Natalie's friends, that he was not the monster the media painted him to be. They had listened to their children on that day, more than three decades ago, tell them where they had been and what had happened. Of course, at that moment in time, they did not know that Natalie was dead. All they could hear were the frantic, breathless rantings of children talking over each other. It was only when they arrived in the woods, seeing her lifeless body in the care of that freak, that they knew the truth. Distraught beyond imagination, they had barely noticed when the police and ambulances arrived to take their child and her killer away. They were oblivious when the other parents crowded together to make sure they were '*all on the same* page'; their children were safely at home, soon to be coached by the grown-ups on what to say when the police inevitably came. *'They were totally innocent. What happened to Natalie was not their fault. The man was crazy. He had shouted at them, lunged at them, grabbed Natalie and kept her. He was dangerous. They were right to run away. Natalie's torn clothes and bruised body were proof of that.'*

Their parents coached them well. The police had needed little encouragement to believe that these children were sweet and innocent. After all, a creepy man had been found in possession of a little girl's body.

They read the newspaper and it brought back such painful memories. They rarely sat together so closely these days. Their divorce, a year after Natalie's 'murder', had not been pretty. On this day, they met up to talk about the past and knew they both needed a cathartic release. There was no-one else they could talk to about what happened all those years ago. No longer in contact with the other children's parents, they only had each other to confide in. Neither one of them really believed that Winter had acted in cold blood, although they did still blame him. The fight to stop him being released on licence had brought them closer together, but they still found it difficult to look each other in the eye. It was too painful. All the other saw was Natalie, and her absence, especially today.

Finally, their eyes lifted from the text, settling on the hot coffee between them. It was finally over. A feeling of relief, happiness or vindication was supposed to wash over them. It never did. Instead, they both felt empty. When they finally spoke to each other, the words were hollow, almost pre-determined. Their daughter's killer was finally dead. This was everything they had wanted for more than half of their lives on earth. Now that it had happened, they both felt almost nothing in response, although neither would admit it. They politely told each other that they could finally move on, regardless of whether the man was truly guilty. It was all his fault and he got the ultimate punishment even if it was by his own hand. Of course, they would still keep in touch, they both affirmed. Of course, they would always be there for the other, they both agreed.

As the former lovers exited the building onto a cold English street, they headed in opposite directions, knowing, of course, that they would probably never see each other again. There was no longer any need. The one thing that had kept them going for so long was finally gone. They needed a new purpose that no longer involved the other.

They had new decisions to make.

Dedication.

Dear Matilda,
Thank you for being you.
I hope you never have to feel the struggle of a tortured mind.
Mummy and Daddy love you more than anything in the world.

You will always be able to tell us anything.

Helplines.

If you would like to read more of this author's work, visit the author's page on amazon.co.uk or any of its international counterparts. If you enjoyed the characters and want to see more of DC Jain or his colleagues, post a review on Amazon or GoodReads and let him know.

If you, or anyone you know, has struggled with anxiety, depression, suicidal ideation or want more advice on any of these topics, visit mind.org.uk. Alternatively, if you need someone to talk to, call The Samaritans on 116 123 for free (UK).

If you're in the US, call 1-800-SUICIDE (1-800-784-2433) or 1-800-273-TALK (1-800-273-8255)

Don't keep it to yourself.

This page is intentionally blank

It was, as with anything in life, a decision.

Printed in Great
Britain
by Amazon